THE STONEHENGE SCROLLS

K.P. ROBBINS

MuseItUp Publishing
www.museituppublishing.com

The Stonehenge Scrolls © 2014 by K.P. Robbins

MuseItUp Publishing
14878 James, Pierrefonds, Quebec, Canada, H9H 1P5
http://www.museituppublishing.com

Cover Art © 2012 by Charlotte Volnek
Edited by Nancy Bell
Copyedited by Judy Roth
Layout and Book Production by Lea Schizas

Print ISBN: 978-1-77127-528-6
eBook ISBN: 978-1-77127-192-9
Production by MuseItUp Publishing

Reviews

"How did the Stonehenge monuments come to be?

"Plenty of nonfiction titles discuss possibilities, but for a fictional perspective that is compelling and involving, you can't beat the thrills and unusual perspectives of *The Stonehenge Scrolls*...a multifaceted, winning novel of prehistory that provides keys not just to Stonehenge and its meaning, but to the lives of the peoples who created it.

"A fine saga. *The Stonehenge Scrolls* is driven by drama and tight, involving writing and is a pick for any who enjoyed Auel's 'Earth's Children' series and similar historical novels."

Midwest Book Review

"I love this book. Framed by the blogging of an archeologist who is amazed at the discovery of ancient scrolls in Ireland which reveal the 'mysterious history of Stonehenge,' we follow the revelation of a long gone society of builders and thinkers. This world of characters and conjecture opens the reader's mind to a well-researched and imaginative possibility.

"After years of her own fascination and study of the subject, Robbins makes this shrouded mystery of the past come alive. Getting drawn in by the story of these fictional 'historic' characters, we feel we may have been in on the secret from the beginning. The unimaginable comes alive. Robbins takes us through the mists of pre-history, and shows us a possibility. It's a great read."

accentBritain.com

Four Stars on Amazon Reader Reviews

For Bill,
my stone-chasing hero,
with love.

From The Washington Press:
IRISH CLAIM TO DISCOVER
SECRETS OF STONEHENGE

WASHINGTON, D.C., May 9—Ancient scrolls revealing the mysterious history of Stonehenge have been discovered in Ireland.

A highway construction crew excavating south of Dublin earlier this year unearthed a sealed bronze chest containing eleven scrolls, written in Latin. At a press conference held yesterday at the National Exploration Society, Irish archaeologist Maeve Haley said radiocarbon testing has established the date of the scrolls as the First Century A.D.

"We have discovered the only written record of what was apparently a longstanding oral tradition," Haley said, "and we plan to assess the details of this storytelling against the known archaeological facts."

When informed of the Irish discovery, leading British archaeologist Nigel Moore expressed skepticism. "Even if the document is authentic—and that's yet to be determined in my opinion—it would have been written thousands of years after Stonehenge was built, which leads one to question its accuracy."

To protect the scrolls during translation, archaeologists carefully unrolled each and placed it in a custom-designed cradle, so its contents could be digitally photographed. Special lighting further protected each manuscript by filtering out ultraviolet rays. The digital images were then enhanced with graphics software, resulting in very legible pages.

The National Exploration Society, which is funding the effort, released the following translation of the introduction to the scrolls:

"I, Oisin, am the last of our priesthood. The profane Romans have killed all my fellow priests and novices. Only I remain here on this island, with just a shallow river separating me from the advancing Roman soldiers."

Haley has surmised that Oisin was a Druid priest on the island of Anglesey in Wales, where the Romans killed off the Druids in the First Century A.D. Latin was the official written language in Britain at that time because of the Roman occupation. Although the Romans chased Britain's Druids to Anglesey, they never ventured to Ireland. Haley pointed out that ferries today still travel across the Irish Sea from Anglesey to the area south of Dublin where the scrolls were found.

Confirming the fact most archaeologists debunk the Druid connection to Stonehenge—the Druids appeared on the scene centuries after Stonehenge was built—Haley speculated, "Perhaps the Druids who recited the stories in these scrolls were actually the descendants of the Stonehenge builders."

Haley acknowledged Stonehenge was built in phases over many centuries, beginning with a circular earthen bank and ditch about 3000 B.C. At first, wooden structures were built there. Fast-forward another four hundred years or so, and stone columns began to be erected within the earthen circle, first some bluestones which were later removed. Finally, around 2500 B.C. the rimmed stone circle of thirty twenty-five-ton uprights was built to surround a horseshoe-shaped arrangement of five 'trilithons,' each consisting of two giant stones weighing as much as forty tons, topped by a third stone weighing fifteen tons. In a final building phase extending over several centuries, a smaller bluestone circle and horseshoe were added inside the larger structures.

"However," Haley said, "what most people today think of as Stonehenge —the rimmed stone circle surrounding the five trilithons—could have been built in one person's lifetime, given the available manpower and technology of that time. Why and how this construction took place is the story told in these scrolls."

Haley said the first scroll describes how the ancient Britons succeeded in moving the giant stones that comprise Stonehenge, some weighing over forty tons. Archaeologists generally agree that these stones were transported from the Marlborough Downs, about twenty miles north of the Stonehenge site.

Reporters pressed Haley for more details on the contents of the scrolls, but she would say only that they are written as if spoken by the four main characters, and these monologues may have once been performed as a means of teaching the Druids their history.

Scroll I

I, Oisin, am the last of our priesthood. The profane Romans have killed all my fellow priests and novices. Only I remain here on this island, with just a shallow river separating me from the advancing Roman soldiers.

For one hundred twenty-five generations, our priests have passed down the stories of the great stone monuments our ancestors built at the Sacred Circle. As a novice, I committed these stories to memory. It took me twenty years to learn them all, and I can still recite them word for word, without omission or error. We were forbidden to put these words into writing, lest our secrets fall into the hands of our enemies. But if the Romans kill me, as I fear they will, the stories of our ancestors will die with me. Already the cursed Romans are claiming our great priestess for themselves, calling her Sulis Minerva.

So I must write. I pray the gods of the Sun and the Moon and the Oak will forgive me for this sacrilege. I will write the stories as I heard them, as I learned to say them. I will write the words of the monument builder Myrddin, who transported the great stones as if by magic; the healer Ogwyn, who cared for the living and the dead; Gwyr, the great chief who united the clans; and most of all, Sulis, whose work will endure forever.

I will begin as I was taught, with Myrddin.

Myrddin

As fast as a clap of thunder, the great-stone, heavier than all the men in the crew combined, careened downhill. The workers who had been pushing it from behind cursed loudly and leapt out of its way, dodging the rolling logs that followed. I watched helplessly as the stone crashed free of the wooden cradle that encased it before finally coming to a stop at the bottom of the hill.

Two hundred men had labored all morning pulling and prodding the great-stone uphill. First the crew levered the stone, steadied by the cradle I had so carefully designed, onto rows of logs. Then two teams of pullers tugged at waist-high ropes tied to the long sides of the cradle as they stepped backward up the hill. Another team, my strongest men, pushed the stone from behind with thick tree limbs. The stone rolled slowly forward, and after it passed over the logs at the back, younger workers raced to move these logs to the front, to keep the stone moving on its rolling bed of logs.

Although generations of Monument Builders had used this method, the one I learned at the Great Tomb on the Boinna River, it wasn't working well on this hilly ground. As the cradle crept uphill, the last log underneath it broke away and began to roll toward the pushers at the back of the stone, who stumbled and fell. Without their support, the weight strained the pullers, who panicked and let go of their ropes.

I studied at Boinna for eleven sun cycles, and then helped erect monuments on the wild western shores of my home island for another two sun cycles. The Master praised my efforts and he himself selected me for this great honor, to take part in constructing Chief Yula's new monument at the Sacred Circle. I did not want to fail in this, my first assignment as a full-fledged Monument Builder.

"I have not given you an easy task, Myrddin," the Master had warned me. "The great-stones each weigh as much as four hundred men, and you must haul them to the Circle from Avlyn, about two days' journey over uneven and hilly land, with local crews not as clever as the people of our island. Although in some ways their backwardness might make it easier to direct them, in other ways, they will make your task more difficult."

As always, the Master was proven correct. The two hundred fifty men and boys I was allotted, fifty from each of the five clans of the Plain, resented having to work with those not of their own clan. I could count on at least one fight breaking out every day. I tried to make their work easier by designing the cradle that held the stone steady, or instructing them to pull by walking backward, instead of forward with ropes slung over their shoulders like dogs. But none of my ideas could compensate for their lack of ability. Not only had a full morning's work been lost, but I knew we would lose the next two days rebuilding the cradle and levering the great-stone back onto the logs before we could try to conquer the hill again.

I glared at the crew in disgust, too angry to speak. Suddenly, as if to match my mood, rolling clouds thundered in the sky. Without a word, I threw my measuring rod to the ground and as soon as I did so, rain began to fall. I strode away in disgust. Behind me, the men were as silent as the dead. I didn't look back at them, and didn't stop walking until I reached my hut in Avlyn. Throwing myself down on my bed of furs, I tried to think.

The rain falling on the thatch roof reminded me of the childhood home I left thirteen sun cycles ago. I was six that summer, when the Master from the Great Tomb on the River Boinna visited our clan in search of boys to train for the brotherhood of Monument Builders. The Master chose me; I didn't know why. Some said he picked boys who showed quickness of mind and body. Others said his choices relied on lineage, and that many Monument Builders had the same telltale reddish hair I was born with. In my mind I pictured the strange wildness of my home as the rain lulled me to sleep.

I dreamed of the thousands of white rocks, like the bones of ancient dragons, which dominated the landscape of my boyhood. I could walk for the entire day and still see their familiar whiteness all around me. I could lie on the rocks and feel their warmth spreading through the length of my body, even in winter. If I looked very closely, I could find hidden entrances to secret underground caves that turned to lakes when the heavy rains came. Tiny flowers grew between the clefts in the rocks, and in my dream I could smell the bright blue and yellow blooms of springtime and the delicate pink, purple, and white petals that magically appeared during winter. At night, the entire landscape glowed like bones held by the priests in the moonlight.

Even these dreams of childhood did not comfort me for long, and I awoke still perturbed by the day's failure. I considered seeking out one of the village girls for comfort. Several had vied for—and received—my attention, but the one who most intrigued me was Ine. I wasn't sure why. Unlike the tall, voluptuous type of woman I was usually attracted to, she was small and thin, with hair and eyes the color of the earth. There was nothing striking about her appearance, yet I was haunted by the smell of lavender in her hair, the smoothness of her skin that tasted like mint, and the confidence in her voice, unafraid to challenge me.

I set off to fetch her from the hut where she lived with her mother, but the old woman, called by the ugly name Ogwyn, stopped me before I reached their doorway. "The blood of the moon is with Ine now, Myrddin," she said. "Leave her be."

Frustrated once again by the bad luck this day had brought me, I decided I needed a cup of mead, which could always be found at the old settlement in the hills north of the village. An ancient track, a wooden path made of cut timbers about an arm's length wide and elevated onto posts where the ground was marshy, marked the route. The ancestors of the local people built many tracks like this over the wetlands and bogs that dotted the Plain to allow travel between their villages.

I found the track slick from the rain, and since I had left my rod at the worksite, I had nothing with which to steady myself. In my overwrought state, I slipped, fell, and then slid at least three strides along the track. My leather tunic and flax cloak afforded some protection, but my calves did not escape a bad scraping. I didn't care. I jumped up with a yelp, not of pain, but of glee.

"That's it," I shouted to the sky. "That's the answer. I'll build tracks to move the stones. No more rolling logs to slow me down." Why hadn't I thought of this solution before? I had wasted too much energy trying to fix the old way instead of devising an entirely new way. I vowed not to make that mistake again.

Early the next morning, I returned to the site to find the men milling around, deliberately avoiding the great-stone. Looking sheepish and somewhat afraid, they gathered around me to await their orders for the day.

"I have a new way to move stones," I announced. "A way that will make your work much easier."

As I explained what I had in mind, building tracks instead of relying on rolling logs, I didn't get the enthusiastic support I'd expected. The workers looked down at the ground and shook their heads, but said nothing, knowing they would have to do what I, the Monument Builder, asked. I had temporarily forgotten how reluctant these Plainsmen were to change from the old ways, all the old ways, even those that meant spending days of work with nothing to show for it.

Finally, the one they called Rudgawr spoke. I had noticed him before, taller than most of his fellow clansmen, almost as tall as myself, and very strong.

"I'm tired of dodging runaway logs uphill and down," he said, to approving laughter. "I think we should try Myrddin's idea. After all, he's just talking about building tracks the way our ancestors have always done."

In that instant I saw Rudgawr would make a good ally.

"All right, Rudgawr, here's what we can do," I replied. "We'll build a short track and see if it's easier to move the great stone on it. And since we need to rebuild the cradle, I'll redesign it to be more like a sled, which will work better on a track. Are you ready to get started?"

Rudgawr clasped my wrist and lifted my arm with his own. "Let's go!" he shouted, and the crew cheered us both.

I dispatched a dozen men to Avlyn to get deer antlers for digging. We needed more logs to build the track, so I chose a hundred men to fell trees and haul them back to the worksite. The rest I set to work with their axes, cutting the log rollers in half lengthwise into planks, and then stripping the bark. At midday, the group returned with the antlers and began digging the trench. Rudgawr and the strongest men pounded the newly dug-out ground with shoulder-high logs, lifting them straight up and bringing them down over and over to harden and flatten the earth.

The digging, pounding, and axe work continued all the next day until finally, we were ready to start laying the track. The men placed the logs, shoulder-width apart and flat side down, into the trench. As had been done on the Plain for generations, they pounded pegs next to the logs to keep them in place and packed small stones and dirt around the outer edges of the log track. I also assigned the best carpenters to build the sled by adding wooden runners to the old cradle design. Since the runners would be the only part of the sled to come into contact with the track, I predicted the sled would move more easily and quickly than the cradle.

At the end of the third day, the track traversed the flat ground approaching the hill, and as the men saw the results of their hard work taking shape, they began to view my plan more favorably. And so, for the next two days they continued to lay the track up the hill. Fortunately the summer weather brought no more thunderstorms. Eager to see if my experiment would succeed or fail, the crew worked with greater energy. I knew bets were being placed, and more against my idea than for it, but I was confident I would succeed.

On the morning of the sixth day, I awoke early, my spirits high with anticipation. I passed by the cook, already tending the fire and roasting pheasants for the midday meal. The cook's helper thrust a small pot under the birds to keep grease from dripping into the fire. I grabbed an apple from his basket and rushed to get another look at the track before the crews arrived.

In the cool, clear morning air, the dark track seemed to shine against the lush green landscape. It was the first thing I had ordered built entirely on my own, without another Monument Builder's instruction. I thought it was beautiful, like a tree reaching toward the sun, except it was horizontal and stretching up the slope. It was only a track, not a monument, but I was still proud of my achievement. I shall always remember that moment as one of the happiest of my life, even better than the excitement that followed.

For it turned out to be a very exciting day, indeed. All the men and boys in the crew, including even the cook and his helper, gathered around to watch as one hundred of my strongest pullers rolled the new sled holding the great-stone over logs and onto the track. I held my breath as the men heaved. The stone moved, but slower than I expected. Again and again they heaved, but with the same slow result. The pullers looked frustrated and disappointed. They, too, had high hopes for my idea, hopes that it would make their task easier. They pulled again as I bent down to examine the track. I saw there was too much scraping of the runners against the track for the sled to move easily. When I glanced up, I caught the eye of the cook's helper, and another inspiration struck me.

"Go, boy," I said to him, "and bring your grease pot from the fireside." When the boy returned, I poured the grease onto the track, and the pullers tried again. The stone lurched forward, a little more quickly, it seemed. They pulled again, and the stone picked up speed. Soon the men were barely tugging at their ropes as the sled with its great-stone moved along the track. The crew cheered as the cook's helper grabbed his pot and ran to pour grease on the track ahead.

The real test came when the stone reached the hill. The men still struggled, but the stone was easier to control on the track than it had been on rolling logs. When the great-stone reached the top of the hill by mid-morning, another cheer arose. Thanks to the new track, we accomplished in half the morning what would have taken a full day with log rollers.

But I wasn't finished with my experiment. Much to the pullers' dismay, I ordered them to move the stone downhill back to its starting point. "I'll put some dirt on the track," I told them, "and that will slow the speed of the sled and make it easier for you to control." Of course, the dirt did as I had predicted, and the stone soon returned to its starting point. By then it was almost mid-day, so I released the crew to their meal and afterward asked the cook's helper to bring me more grease. That afternoon, the men repeated the exercise, moving the stone uphill and down, so I could observe closely and without anticipation.

I sent a messenger to Chief Yula to tell him of my discovery, and, for the next two days, refined my improvements. I had the men smooth the track with their axes to make the surface more even. I tried wet straw and sheep droppings instead of animal fat to make the track slick. Yula arrived on the third day to see for himself.

"You're a magician, Myrddin," he said. "I wouldn't have believed a great-stone could be moved so quickly if I hadn't seen it for myself. The Master Builder told me you were one of his brightest students, but even he will be impressed with your work here."

That night, Yula invited me to his camp near the worksite to eat with him and his lifemate, Aya, a plump, pretty woman. She fed their son Gwyr, who, she told me, was born two winters ago. He was a big baby, tall like his father and strong-willed as well as strong in body. While Aya tended to their son, Yula and I discussed my work.

"Will you need more men to build the track?" Yula asked.

"I can always use more men," I answered. "Especially track builders and rope makers. I can reassign some of the pullers to tree cutting, because the track makes their work easier. Once the track is built, we'll use it again and again. Then you will have several crews taking great-stones to the Sacred Circle at the same time. You should be able to start construction there much sooner than you planned."

"Your ideas are sound, Myrddin, but make sure you're building your track on the best route." I nodded in agreement. Yula was chief not only because of his strength, but also his intelligence.

"There is another path to the Sacred Circle which the older people of Avlyn use," Yula continued, "so you may not know about it. There's only one steep hill on this path—that's why the old people like it—but it's a longer route than the path you've been taking that goes directly from the quarry to the Circle."

"I'll walk both routes myself over the next few days," I promised Yula. "In the meantime, I'll put the crew to work cutting trees and making planks, so we'll be ready to build, whichever route I choose."

"Myrddin, you are always thinking into the future, prepared for anything," said Aya, who had been listening to our conversation. "Tell me, do you ever think of taking a lifemate and fathering a son?"

"My life is dedicated to the brotherhood of Monument Builders, who take care not to father children," I explained. "But I am fond of women and have met some of the girls in Avlyn."

"Tell me who," Aya said. "Perhaps I know them."

"Do you know Ine?"

"Of course. She's the daughter of our clan's medicine woman, Ogwyn."

That was the first time I learned Ogwyn was a medicine woman.

"Ine is a very healthy girl," I replied, thinking of the enthusiasm she brought to our lovemaking.

"Be careful, Myrddin," Aya warned. "Ogwyn could mix a love potion for her daughter, powerful enough to overcome even a Monument Builder."

* * * *

True to my promise to Yula, the next morning I set out to walk the routes. I decided to take Rudgawr with me. As a man from Avlyn, he knew the alternate route Yula described. I also realized I needed a strong ally within the crew, who all regarded me as a suspicious outsider. Rudgawr had their respect, and I wanted to spend time with him to evaluate his character for myself.

We began with the shorter route, since our worksite was located near it. As we approached our first small incline, I bent down and picked up a small pebble from the ground and put it into a leather bag tied to the belt at my waist.

"Why are you gathering stones?" Rudgawr asked.

"This is the way I will remember the number and size of hills along this route," I replied. "I'll put in a small, medium, or large pebble each time we come to a hill. I'll do the same on the other route. This will help me make my choice."

Rudgawr seemed impressed. "I'm glad you asked me to come along with you on your walks," he said. "I think I will learn more than one of your tricks."

The day was sunny and mild, as it usually was here on Yula's Plain, and we made good progress walking at a moderate pace. Along the way, we discussed the route, not only the hills, but also where the cooks could build their fires and set up camp. Shortly after noon, we crossed a stream and came to the River Av that ran south through the Plain.

"Being next to the river is good. We can wash and drink from it," Rudgawr said.

"And we can move our supplies along rafts," I added.

By evening we reached the point where the river crossing was easiest, so we waded to the other side and made camp. By early afternoon the next day, we reached the big bend in the river that marked the spot to turn northwest, uphill to the Sacred Circle. As we climbed, we saw it ahead in the distance. Although I had studied the Sacred Circle during my training at Boinna and visited it twice since arriving on this island, I couldn't help gasping once again in awe and admiration at this most stunning example of ancient earthwork.

Situated slightly higher than the plain that surrounded it, the Sacred Circle was the first project my forefathers, the Monument Builders who preceded me, built for the Clans of the Plain. Thirty generations ago these ancient Monument Builders directed the ancestors of Yula's clansmen as they dug the rocky soil with deer antlers, and then moved basket after basket of dirt and rocks, to construct this circular plot of earth, almost fifty strides across, protected by a ditch. Two high banks made of white chalk, one on either side of the ditch, glittered in the sunlight. I walked past the remaining stone of a pair used to site the midsummer sunrise and stepped into the Circle.

New energy immediately seized my body and mind. I felt the power of the earth rising through the soles of my feet and radiating to my fingertips and the top of my head. I once saw a fellow student at Boinna struck by lightning; he survived, and later tried to describe the experience to us. I never understood it, until I first stepped inside the Sacred Circle.

A work crew was digging out the gray stones erected there several sun cycles ago. I watched as they toppled over a stone taller than they were and proceeded to haul it away. According to Yula's plan, most of the stones now within the earthwork circle would be removed to make way for his new monument, to be built of the great-stones I was struggling to haul here. Only five of the stones would remain, including the large great-stone that marked the chief's place at the ceremonies of life and death. Chief Yula stood before this stone when babies who had survived one full winter, and fewer than half did, were accepted into the clan; when a man and woman pledged to be lifemates; and when the dead were honored. Although I am a tall man, this great-stone was half again my height.

Four smaller stones at the edges of the inner bank would also remain to mark the four corners of the sun-moon rectangle, the great discovery of the current Master Builder. The short sides of the Master's rectangle were in the exact direction of the midsummer sunrise and midwinter sunset. The long sides foretold the moon cycle. This perfect alignment of earth, sun, and moon existed only at the Sacred Circle.

As I left the Sacred Circle, I could feel its energy cleansing and purifying me. I am not a spiritual man. I work with the forces of nature I can touch, like stone, or see, like the sun. I leave the rituals and offerings to the chiefs and their priests. But I must admit that in the Sacred Circle, I feel things I cannot see or touch.

I thought of all the past generations of Monument Builders who had built this place. Their knowledge—of measurements and numbering; circles, squares, and more complex shapes and angles; and the movements of the sun and the moon—defined the Sacred Circle. I admired Yula's ambition to preserve our wisdom in stone. Future generations will marvel at our knowledge embodied in the great-stones that, unlike the wooden temples that once occupied this site, will stand forever.

I spotted Fluj directing some workers on the avenue outside the entrance. As the most senior of the Monument Builders on the Plain, he held the highest honor, overseeing construction at the Sacred Circle. He waved me over.

"Myrddin, I hear you are devising new and faster ways to move the great-stones," he said in greeting. Like most of my fellow Builders, Fluj was a man of few words who got right to the point.

"Yes. I'm building a permanent track to replace the rolling logs. Now I just have to determine the best route. I've spent the past two days traveling one route; now I'll return on an alternate path."

"Don't rush on my account," Fluj replied. "Not only do I have to haul away these stones, but the ancestors of these locals have built so many wooden temples, and huts, and who knows what here. The circle is full of ruts and holes and bones. It's going to take a lot of surveying and earthwork before I can even start construction."

"Don't worry. Whatever the route, I'll need many sun cycles to haul the stones here," I replied.

"And I'll require more sun cycles than I planned to prepare this site because Yula's priest Bolc is constantly halting our work for days at a time," Fluj complained. "Every time Bolc uses the Sacred Circle for his moon rituals and seasonal ceremonies, he disrupts whatever progress I'd made."

I sympathized. "At least I don't have an interfering priest to contend with."

Rudgawr and I spent the night in Fluj's work camp, and then started back to Avlyn by the alternate route in the morning. It was, as Yula described, a much easier way, mostly over flat ground, but it took us two full days to reach Avlyn, instead of a day and a half. "This is a much easier route," Rudgawr said, "and only a half-day longer."

I smiled at his ignorance. "Yes, if we could haul the great-stones as fast as we can walk," I replied. I did a quick calculation in the dirt before I continued. "But I calculate that with this route it would take much longer to haul all the stones, at least three sun cycles longer. And without the river nearby, we would have to haul water as well, leaving fewer men to haul stone. So even with more hills, the shorter route is better."

Rudgawr's face reddened and the veins in his neck tightened. "You're not of our clans," he said, "so you don't care how hard it is for us to haul great-stones up hills, even with your tracks."

I was taken aback by Rudgawr's outburst. I needed him on my side. "I haven't made up my mind yet," I told him. "And you are right; I must consider the men doing the hauling. Let's walk the routes again, together, and discuss it some more." Rudgawr nodded.

And so the next day we started out again on the shorter route. This time, we didn't talk much. At sunset we camped on the riverbank, at the same spot as before. From the place behind my navel came the deep knowing that this was the route to choose, but I couldn't think of the reasons to convince Rudgawr. Tired and bored, I picked up a pebble, flung it into the river, and watched as it sank. My thoughts drifted to images of Ine's lithe body and firm breasts. I remembered our last coupling, how she cried out and how she clung to me afterward. My mouth watered, and in frustration I threw another pebble and then another. A piece of bark floated by, and I tossed a bit of stone onto it.

The pebble didn't sink, but floated on the bark. Immediately I saw the answer I had been seeking.

"Rudgawr," I said. "What if, instead of hauling the stones along this path, we float them along the river, just like we'd float the supplies. That would save your men a lot of effort, wouldn't it?" Since most of the short route was along the river, the men would have to haul the great-stones over land only at the beginning of our journey and at the very end, up from the river to the Sacred Circle.

Rudgawr's mouth fell open, and his eyebrows shot up. "It would certainly be easier if we could move the stones part of the way along the river," he admitted. "But wouldn't the great-stones sink? They weigh so much more than supplies."

Instead of answering, I asked, "Do you know Corna, the Monument Builder who directs the stone cutters?"

"Yes, I know who he is."

"Well, Corna and I trained together, and we came to your island from across the sea on a boat that held ten men and many supplies. If we could float, then perhaps a great-stone can be made to float."

"Myrddin, I hope your magic is powerful enough to float a great-stone," Rudgawr replied.

Although I was pleased with myself for again thinking of a new way to accomplish our task, I wanted to discuss this idea with Corna. His mind worked differently than mine. While I often raced to a certain conclusion without being able to explain why, Corna analyzed the reasons that supported my direct knowing. In my mind, I could hear him repeating the words of our teachers at Boinna: "Do not be afraid to make a mistake, so long as it is a new mistake, one no Monument Builder has ever made before."

I told Rudgawr we wouldn't take the old people's path again, but instead return directly to Avlyn in the morning to meet with Corna. I didn't mention my other reason for wanting to hurry back: to see Ine again. I missed the adventuresome energy she brought to our lovemaking. We coupled in every way possible, lying on my bed, or me taking her from behind, or Ine standing against a tree. Clever and determined, she was the most exciting girl I had ever known. I would search her out right after I saw Corna.

* * * *

I found Corna at the stone fields with his crew of cutters, pounding stone against stone to smooth and shape the building blocks I would eventually haul. Despite the hard, noisy work, the men respected Corna. Although small in stature, he was strong and fearless. I had known this since our boyhood together.

Corna and I first met near the Great Tomb at Boinna, where a large circle of wooden stakes stood atop the hillside. Inside the circle, an old man with orange and white hair, like a cat I once had, presided. He was our teacher, a Monument Builder named Doul, and Corna and I were two of his seven novices, seven being one of the favored numbers of the Monument Builders.

In those first days of our training, Doul taught us the story of the brotherhood for which we had been chosen. Each day, he made us repeat his words, and he refused to continue until every boy could recite the story correctly. Thus we learned how the Monument Builders studied the movements of the moon and the sun and the energy in the earth and in lakes, rivers, and seas. Doul shared this knowledge passed down for more than one hundred fifty moon journeys. We learned each journey of the moon across the horizon took almost nineteen sun cycles to complete, about as long as we novices would have lived by the time we completed our training.

Doul showed us how to predict the movements of the sun. We observed the rising and setting sun each day and recorded our observations on the wooden stakes surrounding our teaching circle. Soon we came upon a day when light and darkness were equal, neither summer nor winter. Doul explained there were two perfect "even days" each sun cycle, powerful days, but not the most powerful. "Depending on which priest you believe," Doul said, "the most powerful day is either the midsummer sunrise, the longest day of every sun cycle, or its opposite, the midwinter sunrise, the shortest day."

On the first midwinter sunrise we spent at Boinna, Doul awakened Corna, me, and the other boys in the middle of the night. "Now is when your new life begins," he said as he led us to the Great Tomb. As we approached it, I noticed something different in the dim moonlight. The slab sealing the doorway to the tomb was moved to the side. The Master stood between the open doorway and the huge horizontal stone, beautifully carved with spirals, that guarded the entrance.

"Climb over the spirals and join me," he called to us.

Not knowing what to expect, we novices did as the Master ordered. Although the tallest, I was barely able to mount the huge stone. Doul lifted Corna and the others up. When we were all gathered before the doorway, the Master said, "Follow me if you wish to become a Monument Builder," and entered the tomb. I had never been inside this, or any tomb before, and the hair on my neck stood up as dread coursed through me. Nevertheless, I fell into line, the first behind him with Corna close behind me. As I stumbled up the narrow passageway, I felt the cold stones so close to my body on either side, but saw nothing in the total blackness.

We walked about forty steps before stopping at what felt like an open space, and the Master told us to wait. We stood still in the suffocating darkness, not knowing what was to happen next. I held my hand in front of my face, but could see nothing. One of the boys wet himself, and I recognized the smell of fear as well as urine. For the first time in my life, I was truly terrified and groped for Corna's hand.

"Don't be afraid, Myrddin," he whispered.

As I clutched his hand tightly, I heard a few muffled sobs from the others. Just when I thought I could bear my fright no longer, a beam of light appeared from above. As it traveled down the path through which we had just come, I saw spirals carved on the stones that lined the passageway. The light must be coming in from the rising sun, I concluded, captured in the tomb the Monument Builders had made generations before. The sunlight filled the space in which we stood. I saw we were in a circular room with three chambers, each about as wide and deep as I was tall. The Master pointed out carvings on their walls and ceilings, carvings all the more beautiful because they were hidden from the view of outsiders. In each chamber stood a stone basin holding bones, the bones of Monument Builders who had come before us, the Master said.

No longer frightened, I released Corna's hand and looked up at the magnificent roof unlike any I had ever seen before, made not of branches, grass or turf, but of layered slabs of stone. At that instant, I knew I wanted to build great monuments like this one. When the light inside the tomb began to fade, the Master said, "As you once exited your mother's womb to be born into the world, go forth from this tomb to be reborn to your new life as a

Monument Builder." Thus ended the first of many tests we novices would endure to prove our courage and ability to think clearly.

From that day, Corna and I stayed close to each other. Now I needed his help again. He saw me approaching and came forward to greet me.

"Myrddin, my brother, what brings you here?"

I quickly explained my idea to float the great-stones down the River Av. "Tell me, Corna, do you think it's possible?"

He replied in his usual cautious way, and I knew from experience to keep silent until he completed his thoughts.

"It depends. You'll have to build a raft big enough and strong enough to hold the great-stone. That shouldn't be a problem, since you're already building sleds from ash to haul the great-stone over land. Maybe you can just slip the sleds into the river." Corna paused to consider what he had just recommended before continuing. "Will ash float with a great-stone on it? I'd say you'd have to use a lighter wood. Pine is light, and plentiful, and easy to fell."

I nodded. As usual, Corna had raised the specific questions I needed to consider. "Whatever wood you use," he continued, "the raft would have to be much wider than the stone, just like your pebble and piece of bark. While a boat with men and supplies floats on the sea, the sea is much deeper than this river."

Corna's thoughts seemed to have run out, but I wasn't satisfied. "I know the river is not as deep as the sea, but the great-stone doesn't have to float close to the surface of the water, as a boat with men does," I answered. "The great-stone has to float just enough so that it doesn't run aground. It can be helped along with ropes pulled by men walking along the river banks."

"Well then, Myrddin, let's build a model, like we learned at Boinna, and see what depth we need to float a great-stone. Then you can measure the depth of the river, and you'll know for sure if the water route will work."

The next day Corna and I selected a stone for our experiment, one as thick as a typical great-stone, but only as long as a man's arm, about one builder's length and about half again as wide. While Corna took on the task of designing a raft and supervising its construction, I instructed Rudgawr to take two men and measuring sticks and go to the river. There they were to build a small raft and proceed down the Av, measuring and marking its depth on measuring sticks every tenth raft length. While Rudgawr took the measurements, his helpers were to throw out a stone anchor and use poles to hold the raft as still as possible.

"Well, that will measure the water now, but it's deeper after the winter storms and the rains of the planting season," Rudgawr said. "So will we go back then and measure again?"

"Good question," I replied, although I hated to admit to Rudgawr I hadn't thought of this myself. I made a quick decision. "Measure now. It's easier when the water is low. If we do move the stones by water, we'll do it when the water is highest. You and your men have observed the River Av through many seasons, and I have not. Tell me, Rudgawr, how much deeper does it get after the rains?"

He seemed pleased to be able to tell me something I didn't already know. "I have seen the Av flood its banks when I was a child, and again after I first began working for Chief Yula six summers ago. But usually, I would say the water rises about this much," he said, holding one hand palm down at his neck and one palm up at his navel, about half a builder's length.

I cut a line onto one of the measuring sticks with a piece of flint. "If you find some spots where the water is below this line, mark the place on the riverbank."

Within a few days, Corna designed and built a pine raft, about twice as wide as, and slightly longer than, the small stone. A crew carried it to the village pond, which had a depth of one builder's length, lashed the stone to the raft and pushed it into the pond. It promptly sank. Some of the crew gasped, and a few laughed. Corna looked more puzzled than upset. "Myrddin," he said, "we have a problem."

Corna and I retired to my hut to discuss it. I lay down on the furs of my straw bed, where I always did my best thinking. Corna paced back and forth, talking through the facts of the problem, just as we had been taught.

"We know stone doesn't float and wood does," he said. "We know that stones placed on wood will float, but for this to happen, first the design has to be right, and then the water has to be deep enough. So either my design is wrong, or we need to test it in a deeper pond."

I smiled, admiring the order of his thoughts, but my mind had already jumped forward. "If we can't make a stone this size float in the depth of the pond, we won't be able to make a real great-stone float in the river. Remember what we learned at Boinna about increasing and decreasing measurements in models; if you increase one measure, the others must change in the same proportion. The real great-stone is about one hundred times heavier than our test stone, but the river is maybe only ten times deeper than the pond. If we can't make our test stone float in the pond, a great-stone isn't going to float in the river."

"So, it's back to my design for the raft," said Corna. "If the water can't be deeper, the raft needs to be bigger. I'll make it wider."

"A wider raft will probably work," I said. "But remember, our test stone is smaller than the real great-stone, so when we build the real raft, it will be many times wider. A wider raft would do on the sea, but not on the Av, which is narrow even for a river."

"Well, then, maybe the water route won't work," Corna said. "We can't make the raft wider than the river itself, and I've never seen a boat, let alone a raft, much longer than a great-stone."

We sat silently for a while. What Corna said made sense, but I was reluctant to forget the water route. The raft couldn't be wider or longer, but— and then inspiration struck—it could be deeper. "What if we built two rafts, lashed them together, and put them under the stone?" I proposed to Corna. "We can make the raft bigger that way."

"Yes, but why do you think it would float?"

"Because wood floats. We need enough of the floating, upward force of wood to overcome the weight of the stone. With enough wood it will float; we saw that with the pebble and bark. Since we can't build the raft wider or longer, we must build deeper. Let's try it and see."

And so we returned to the pond, where the crew was still loitering, and had them pull the raft and stone out. Then Corna set the men to building a second raft. The next day, we tried our experiment again, this time with two rafts lashed together, one on top of the other. The stone floated and bobbed in the pond, and the crew cheered. Corna shook his head in disbelief.

"Myrddin, I wouldn't have believed it if I hadn't seen it myself. We added more weight, more wood, and the cursed stone floats. How do you think of these things? It's magic."

"No, not magic. I leave that to the priests. I rely only on my training, and observation, and thinking. Now let's add some weight to see how much the double raft will hold without sinking."

For the rest of the day and the next, we added another stone and then another. Each time the raft sank deeper in the water, but it still floated above the bottom of the pond. I marked on measuring sticks how far the raft sank with each added weight. Even as it sank lower in the water, the men could stand on either side of the pond and, with ropes tied to the raft, pull it back and forth with ease. Finally, we added one too many stones and the raft stuck in the mud at the bottom of the pond. But by that time, I had all the measurements I needed. If the river was at least three lengths deep, a triple raft five lengths wide and ten lengths long would float a great-stone. Now all I needed were Rudgawr's measurements.

Several days later, Rudgawr returned with his measuring sticks. The marks on the stick ranged from just under two lengths to about four lengths. Even with the additional half-length of water I could expect from the winter rains, the sticks showed the river wasn't deep enough in three places. I thanked Rudgawr for his good work, but told him we would have to move the stones over land.

"Why?" he asked. "I hear from my clansmen you can get heavy stones to float on a double raft. Why not use the river? It will be a lot easier on the men."

"Because the water has to be deep enough, at least as high as this," I said, pointing to the mark I had cut on the measuring stick before he set out. "And as your own marks show, there are three places where the water isn't that deep."

"We can make the water deeper by building dams, just like we do to irrigate our fields," Rudgawr answered. Once again, his local knowledge proved valuable.

"That might work. Can you show me where you found the shallow water?"

"Yes. As you instructed, I built a small mound of rocks along the river bank where the water was below your line."

And so, for the third time, Rudgawr and I walked the short route together. When we reached the river, he found his raft and we set off on the water. I periodically jumped into the water to verify Rudgawr's measurements. In places where the water was over my head, I knew we would have no trouble floating the great stone. But at the shallow places Rudgawr marked, I could stand on the river bottom and still see, with my eyes barely above the surface of the water. But with damming, as Rudgawr suggested, the stones could be transported on the river.

I knew I was right about this. Even as a boy, I excelled at measurements and computations, at calculating circles with the secret twenty-two/seven number of the Monument Builders and predicting the success of larger structures by making smaller models. I could confidently inform Yula I had discovered the quickest route to move the stones.

I have written all day to record this long soliloquy. I remember struggling with it as a lad. I didn't really understand it all at the time, especially the references to lovemaking. It took me a full year to learn, but Myrddin's character inspired me. Looking back on it, I think that's why this was the first story taught us, for inspiration to face our problems and solve them. And also to eliminate, from the very beginning, those boys with poor memories.

Our next assignment was easier, the cures of the medicine woman Ogwyn.

Maeve Haley's Blog

Ever since the press conference announcing the discovery of the scrolls, I have been besieged with inquiries from the media, my fellow archaeologists, and interested members of the general public. So I have decided to launch this blog in the hope that I can address the questions and issues raised by these amazing documents.

Stonehenge Architects Were Irish
Posted July 29

It's fortuitous that the Stonehenge scrolls were discovered near Dublin—and that I was given the assignment to evaluate their contents—because there's just no doubt in my mind that Myrddin's home island was Ireland.

As an Irish archaeologist who values my country's rich prehistory (and as a woman), I'm sure my conclusions won't always agree with those of Professor Nigel Moore, the English expert who acknowledges Ireland only as an insignificant part of "the British Isles." But even Mr. Moore cannot doubt the Monument Builders' school Myrddin describes is Ireland's Newgrange on the Boyne River. Even after five millennia, I think Myrddin himself would still recognize it.

As Mr. Moore will undoubtedly point out, I can't definitively prove there was a designated group of architects, engineers, and general contractors like the Monument Builders that had a training school. But the idea seems a historical precedent to the guilds in the Middle Ages, or even our universities today. If the Monument Builders did exist, their headquarters would have been at Newgrange. Even though not at all centrally located at the very western edge of Europe, Newgrange was the center of the action in Neolithic times, as evidenced by the wealth of beautifully carved stones there and at nearby Knowth and Dowth in the Boyne Valley. Several centuries older than the stone circle at Stonehenge, Newgrange hints that the Irish may have *started* western civilization, not just saved it.

Thousands visit this World Heritage site north of Dublin every year, and I'd say the average tourist would find the huge reconstructed tomb there more impressive than the ruined circle at Stonehenge. Newgrange boasts an impressive (if reconstructed) white quartz facade, a roof that hasn't leaked in five thousand years, and of course, that magical bit with the midwinter sunrise illuminating the inner chamber. People used to reserve years in advance to go inside the tomb at Newgrange during the winter solstice, even though if it was cloudy and rainy like it usually is in Ireland, they wouldn't see a thing. Now a lottery determines who gets in; fifty winners, each permitted to bring one guest, are chosen every year. Last year's lottery drew over thirty-four thousand entries.

And Myrddin's description of his home, of the white rocks dominating the landscape? Sounds just like the Burren, a unique limestone formation that covers acres in County Clare. Orchids do bloom there in the winter, just as Myrddin describes. Seeds were deposited during the Ice Age, and the limestone retains enough heat to allow orchids to grow.

The Route of the Stones
Posted July 31

Ted M. asks: "I've been looking at some maps of England and Myrddin's land-and-river route for hauling the stones seems feasible. What do you think?"

I agree.

Over the years, several archaeologists have experimented with teams of young students pulling stones over rolling logs. In 1979, a group in France moved a thirty-two-ton block with two hundred people. When the experiment was repeated again in 1997 with improved techniques, it took one hundred twenty men to move the block. With further engineering refinements—but limited to tools and materials that would have been available in 2500 BC— only ten men were needed to move the huge stone.

The builders of Ireland's Newgrange, constructed five hundred years before Stonehenge, probably transported heavy stones on the River Boyne, a fact that Myrddin, trained at Newgrange, probably knew, although he doesn't admit it in these scrolls.

The River Avon isn't an impressive river, a big stream, really, not more than a hundred feet wide at its broadest point. If huge stones had traveled along this river, men with long poles could have guided their passage from parts of the shoreline.

Scroll II

Ogwyn

Ine, my daughter, has crossed the chalk line into the world of the dead in the most glorious way a woman can. Her death has given new life to another girl child. As medicine woman to the dead and the living, I care for both my daughter and my granddaughter now. Honoring the dead protects the living.

Even as a child, I did not fear the dead. I harvested the bones of the dead in the wooden charnel house at the top of the hill and prepared them for burial in the long barrow, the one guarded by stones to keep the spirits of the dead inside. We used many plants and flowers in the preparations, and I soon began to see that their effect was not only on smell. The dead led me to study plants for the living.

I make a dandelion brew for the colds that come with the rains. I use nettles to numb the skin when a cyst must be cut. I know the flowers a woman must eat after a mating she has changed her mind about, to cause her bleeding of the moon again, my most popular cure.

I wish Ine had asked me for that cure. But instead she wanted a love potion to capture Myrddin, the Monument Builder. All the girls in the village were taken with him, his long stride, his restless activity, and his hair the color of leaves before they fall from the trees. If I were half my age, fifteen winters like Ine was when she asked me for the potion, I might have pursued Myrddin myself!

It was not easy to give Ine what she asked for. As a Monument Builder, Myrddin knew the cycles of the moon and when to stay away from a woman. But my old ways overcame his new ways. I mixed the crushed petals of clovers and leaves of mint with some flaxseed oil and rubbed it into Ine's skin, to relax her and make her even more attractive to the Monument Builder. I told Ine to save her blood of the moon, and I mixed it with the dried pink flowers of my most favored healing plant and a root that has power to provoke a man's desire and strengthen his seed. Ine secretly stirred this potion into the mead she offered Myrddin. Very soon, it was clear our plan had worked, and her belly began to grow with child.

But the dead punished me for deceiving their Monument Builder. They took Ine for themselves. The birthing was long with much blood, all my medicines powerless to help her. Her body, too small and too taut, like a twig easily snapped, was not made for childbirth. So now, in my old age of thirty-two winters, I must rear a girl child again. I promise the dead I won't make the same mistakes I made with Ine.

Myrddin

Why has this girl child bewitched me so?

I shouldn't have named her, for naming recognized my bond with her. But I didn't want her to have a harsh name like Ine, her mother, or Ogwyn, her grandmother, so I called her Sulis, a soft and pleasing sound.

Sulis. Maybe it's the name, maybe it's the child herself, but I am enchanted with every simple thing she does. Her first tentative steps, her baby babbling, how she tries to say my name—these ordinary actions seem amazing when she does them. Every time I see her, I marvel at how much she's changed and grown since my last visit. And then she wants *me* to hold her. I, Myrddin the Monument Builder, do not hold children, but when she cries and puts her arms out to me, tears—tears!—come to my eyes, and I must lift her up, if only to hide my emotion.

I am a man of learning. I know the sacred numbers and measurements of which these local simpletons are ignorant. I know where the sun will rise in the sky tomorrow and when the moon will be full again. I have made men do work they thought could not be done. Although I am a powerful man on these Plains, I am powerless to resist this beautiful child.

I have slept with many women, as I did with Ine, her mother, and I have always been careful to time my sexual adventures with the moon, to avoid getting the woman with child. Fatherhood is not fitting for those who have monuments to build. But the old witch Ogwyn, Ine's mother, knows the ways of plants. She must have given Ine something to make her particularly fertile around the time of the Even Day festival, when the village celebrated the end of the harvest. Or perhaps Ine put something in the festival mead to make my seed stronger. Maybe both. And so I became a father, and Ine died in the birth.

There's no doubt the child is mine. The local people all have dark hair. She has hair the reddish gold of the setting sun, the sign of a Monument Builder.

* * * *

"You'll spoil that girl, Myrddin," Ogwyn said. "Not even the great Chief Yula can name the day of his birth. All I know about my own birth is that I was born sometime between the winter festival and the planting moon."

"Well, you weren't born on the longest day of the sun cycle," I replied. "That's certainly a day worth noting, the day with the most light and the least darkness."

What I didn't tell Ogwyn was that the day of Sulis' birth foretold great things for her. As a girl, she was a child of the moon, but her birth-day put her under the sun's special protection as well.

"Myrddin, did you bring me something?" Sulis asked.

"Yes, I have a surprise for your third birth-day," I answered, as Ogwyn rolled her eyes in disgust. "Whoever heard of a gift to remember a birth-day?" I heard her mutter.

I took Sulis outside, away from Ogwyn's disapproval, to receive her present. It was a dog of the kind found around Avlyn, with long legs and big feet, an intelligent looking face with a long snout, and short, wiry hair, both black and brown. We called them tomb dogs, because they were good at digging. Since I was often gone, I thought Sulis needed some companionship other than the old woman. I hoped the dog would keep rats and squirrels out of their hut, but looking at the jumping, whimpering puppy, I wondered if he would be of any use at all.

"Oh, he's so funny, Myrddin. He trips over his own big feet. And he must like me, because he's jumping into my lap. I'm going to call him Cwimgwily."

"Hey, I'm the Monument Builder. I do the naming around here."

"No, I'm calling him Cwimgwily. It's a silly name, and he's a silly puppy. I like the name. I can name things, too, Myrddin, because when I grow up, I'm going to build monuments like you do. Ogwyn says I have the hair of a Monument Builder."

Well, what else could I do? I was so proud she wanted to be like me, I let her call the dog what she wanted, and I didn't tell her that no women were Monument Builders.

Sulis

The sky and sun protect me, like my mother's arms they enfold me, the arms of the mother I never knew. The breeze soothes me and whispers in my ear, like the voice of the mother I never knew. I feel safe here, near my mother's bones.

When Ogwyn is busy with her plants and her cures, I come here with Cwimgwily. I like walking down the hill through the two rows of giant stones. They are guarding me, keeping me on the right path, telling me, "Sulis, you belong in this place. Stay inside this place." Where the rows of stones end, I turn toward the Great Mound Hill my people made many generations ago and walk toward it. I pass it and climb to the top of the hill, and there is my little double circle of stones, open to the sky. In my village, huge stones surround us, spread out in circles like sentries. Here the stones are small, the circles are small, just the right size for me.

Ogwyn says there used to be a wooden shelter here, when she was my age, where she helped the medicine women and the priests prepare the dead for their burial in the Long Tomb on the other side of the hill. The building is gone now; I don't know why. The stone circles were erected to honor the dead whose bones were once sheltered here. That's why Ogwyn calls this place the Shelter.

Nearby are three burial mounds. My mother's bones are buried in one of them. Myrddin, my father, had them put there because the mounds are near the path over which many of his tools and supplies come. He says he will be reminded of her spirit often, because he will be here anyway, to get his supplies. That's the way my father does things.

I don't do everything exactly like my father, although he wants me to. I come here to be near my mother's bones, yes, but also because it feels like the top of the world. I like to stand on this high hill, and look up at the sky, and spin round and round in circles. It's always windy here, and my spinning catches the wind. I keep spinning, and I can look out over the hills and valleys and fields and trees, those I know and those so far away I don't know them.

As I spin, I feel the sun's warmth on my arms, I smell the little yellow flowers in bloom, I hear the noisy chirping of the birds. Finally, I collapse from all that spinning. I am alive. Here, in what once was a Shelter for the dead, I am alive, in touch with the earth and the sky.

And when I'm here at the top of my world, I can see how the sun makes shadows next to the stones, and how the shadows change throughout the day, and are different in different seasons.

When I told Myrddin this, he seemed very pleased. "Sulis," he said with a rare grin on his face, "perhaps you have inherited more than your red hair from me. You have keen powers of observation."

"Yes, Myrddin, my father," I answered, "and one day I can help you in your work, if you teach me."

Myrddin thought for a while before replying, "Sulis, monument building is men's work."

"The stone hauling, yes," I said, "but it does not take strength to observe or to measure as I have seen you do." I climbed into his lap and put my arms around his neck. "Please. Ogwyn teaches me about her work, her plants. I want to learn your work, too. Please."

Myrddin smiled down at me. "Well, what harm would it do?" he said, and from that day I began to learn the Monument Builders' secrets.

My father teaches me how to count and how to use his measuring rod. He instructs me to watch where the sun rises and sets and to observe the waxing and waning of the moon. "These are things Monument Builders must know, so we can place the stones in just the right place," Myrddin told me. "And I first learned them at Boinna, when I was just six sun cycles, about your age."

My father often tells me stories of his boyhood across the sea. He says the stones of the Great Tomb there are carved. I have never seen carvings on stone, and my father draws the symbols for me in the dirt. "Spirals for water energy, squares for earth energy, circles for the sun and life, zigzags for the moon and death. Remember these symbols, Sulis, and tell no one their meaning."

My father says that when I am older, he will teach me how to find the energies and measure their strength. He said that at Boinna, the priests dug holes in the stone carvings and inserted their magic rods to capture their energy. I was fascinated by this idea, but my father was skeptical. "I knew we

Monument Builders could find the energy, but I was never convinced the priests could capture it as they claimed, any more than I could hold onto a ray of sunlight," he said.

"Ogwyn says the old priest Bolc, who died before I was born, used to bless the stones. She says stones are sacred," I told him.

"I don't know if stones are sacred," Myrddin replied, "but unlike plants, animals, and men, stones do not grow old. Nor do they die. Stone does not decay, like wood, nor does it wash away, like mud. That's why Monument Builders rely on stone."

Sometimes, when I don't know the solution to a problem my father has posed for me, I listen to his thoughts to find the answer. I haven't told Myrddin I can hear his thoughts. My mother's people, who have powers unshared even by Monument Builders, passed on this gift to me.

Only a few clan chiefs or priests know some of the things my father is teaching me, but most do not. I want to know everything my father knows, the knowledge the Monument Builders do not share with anyone, not even Chief Yula. I am Myrddin's only child. He and his thoughts cannot deny me.

So you can see, dear reader, that the child Sulis already showed great power. Even Myrddin, who commanded crews of tough clansmen, could not resist her. Perhaps it was only a father's love that made him yield to her, or perhaps it was the genius of Sulis herself. Among all the learned professions of our priesthood, neither poets nor physicians, neither prophets nor advisers to kings, possess her power to read minds.

But Myrddin had responsibilities other than Sulis, important work to do, as I will tell you next. I have plenty of daylight left to continue writing.

Maeve Haley's Blog

Scrolls Consistent With Other Ancient Legends
Posted August 2

It's not the kind of proof that would satisfy Professor Nigel Moore, but I'm intrigued that another story seems to verify these scrolls.

In the twelfth century Geoffrey of Monmouth, famous for recording the King Arthur tales, wrote that Merlin magically transported the stones used to construct Stonehenge from Ireland to the Salisbury Plain. I think Geoffrey was recording a bit of folk memory, and in some strange way this bit of misinformation lends credence to the scrolls. First, I think I've established that Myrddin was born in Ireland, and the ingenious methods he devised to move the stones probably did seem magical to the average person of his day. Most interesting to me, given my Gaelic ancestry, is that the Welsh name for Merlin is Myrddin.

But one name isn't just legend; it's quite literally carved in stone. Twenty-five centuries after the stone circle was built, the Romans constructed their famous baths at Bath, England, now a short drive from Stonehenge. The dedication over the entrance reads: Sulis Minerva. The tour guides there will tell you the latter was a Roman goddess, but the former, a local goddess powerful enough for the Romans to honor.

Avebury
Posted August 3

It occurs to me that Sulis and Ogwyn could have lived near the modern-day village called Avebury, not too far from Stonehenge and still surrounded today by giant stone circles from Neolithic times. At Avebury a double row of stones leads down a hill, perhaps the path followed by Sulis to her Shelter, which coincidentally (or not) sounds like a nearby site archaeologists call the Sanctuary. Opposite it, at the crest of the hill, stand a few small burial mounds alongside a prehistoric path now called the Ridgeway. Perhaps one of those mounds once held Ine's bones.

Scroll III

Myrddin

For nine sun cycles I oversaw the hauling of stones to the Sacred Circle. Yula arranged for each clan to give me one hundred fifty able-bodied men and fifty boys, barely into their teens. Altogether I had a thousand men and boys to feed and keep busy, and they moved no stones the summer Sulis was born. Instead, the men built tracks and dams, the sled and the raft, while the boys braided bark into ropes, cut small trees for guide sticks, fished and hunted for food, and carried supplies to the campsites.

Many days, however, far fewer workers than I needed showed up. "No matter what the chiefs have pledged to Yula, these men need to tend their own crops and animals so their families will be fed," Rudgawr explained. At harvest time, Rudgawr persuaded me to send the men home. "They'll come back," he promised (and most did), "and when they do, you'll have their full attention." Once again, Rudgawr's advice stood me in good stead.

By the time of the first full moon after the harvest, enough track had been laid so hauling could begin. I assigned one hundred of the strongest men to the task, and we made another fortuitous discovery: the stone moved easier along a frosty track. The men moved faster, too, in the colder weather, perhaps to keep warm or perhaps because they had fewer worries about their crops. By late spring, we had succeeded in hauling one great-stone over the newly built track all the way to the River Av, at its highest after the rains. Now it was time to roll the stone over logs onto the raft and set it on its journey downstream toward the Sacred Circle.

The day of the launch, Corna came to watch. Although I could sense his excitement, he remained his calm, deliberate self.

"That triple raft is much larger than I somehow imagined it would be, and with the great-stone on top of it—do you really think it will float, Myrddin?" he asked.

"You haven't forgotten our experiment, have you? I've checked my calculations many times. It will float," I assured him.

Corna watched as the men lashed the stone to the raft. "Make sure they encircle the stone many times, and tie the rope tightly," he advised. "You don't want the stone to slide off when the raft enters the water."

Boys were spreading grease over the track, which traversed a short slope down to the river.

"That was another good idea you had, Myrddin, to add runners to the raft, to make it easier to launch," Corna said.

The men began pulling the raft and stone over the track, and when they reached the point at which the track sloped downward, I instructed them to stop pulling and push from behind instead. They put their shoulders into it, grunting and straining, and finally the raft moved just far enough so that it tipped over onto the slope, and its own enormous weight propelled it into the river with a great splash that obstructed our view.

"Did it sink?" a boy asked.

"It's floating, it's floating," Corna cried, as we watched the top of the stone bob up and down in the water. Onshore, the crew jumped and cheered. Four young men quickly swam to the other side of the narrow river, picked up the long poles that had been left on the river bank for them, and followed the raft downstream. They prodded the raft with their poles to keep it floating in the deep center of the Av. Four more carried poles into the shallow water on my side of the bank, ready to push the raft to the center if it drifted too far toward them. Once the raft reached its destination, another crew of one hundred men would have to bring it ashore and haul it uphill over another recently built track to the Sacred Circle.

That night, Corna and I celebrated my accomplishment with the local mead. Although our ways of thinking differed, we each appreciated the other's ideas. In some ways, we were like brothers, raised together from boyhood and now continuing our work far from our home island.

By Sulis' third birthday, only three great-stones had been moved to the Circle. Along the way, the crew's carelessness caused accidents and injuries, despite my best efforts. In most cases, their own rowdy behavior, fighting and drinking were to blame. Six drowned, only one while performing his work duties. Three were crushed under the heavy stones. Broken limbs, wounds, and cuts too numerous to count arose daily. When a severely injured man returned home, his chief didn't always feel obligated to send a replacement.

Despite that, the men and I got better at our task. I refined the design of the sled and raft, and the men devised among themselves ways to work more safely. By the end of the fourth summer, we had moved two more great-stones, and we continued at that rate of two great-stones for the next several summers. By the end of the eighth summer, we moved an additional three great-stones, an incredible achievement.

There was only one more stone to haul, but when I returned to Avlyn that fall, I learned that final stone came at a great price. The quarry workers somehow lost control and let the great-stone fall, killing Corna. The story the workers told me, the details of the accident they described, did not console me. The man I had known for most of my life, the brother I could always count on, was gone. They buried his bones in a burial mound near Ine's. I had no one to turn to for solace, except my daughter.

I didn't want to leave Sulis (who had by now celebrated eight birth-days) after my work here was completed. Despite being a girl, she had inherited some of my aptitude. She herself recorded, without any prompting on my part, the movements of the sun at various times of the year. She begged me to teach her numbers and computations. "What use will that be to you?" I protested and she replied, "So I can help you in your work, Myrddin, when I grow up." I knew such a thing would never happen, but I loved her for the thought. Perhaps it was foolish of me to indulge her, but Sulis was such an outstanding pupil. Besides, what did I know about raising a girl child? I could teach her only what I knew, so I taught her what I learned at Boinna when I was her age.

I knew I was fortunate to work for Chief Yula, who was pleased with my progress. "You've done in my lifetime what would have taken two generations in my father's day," he said. I had come to admire Yula's skills, although different from those of Monument Builders. He envisioned a bigger and more impressive monument to display the wealth and power of all the Clans of the Plain and convinced the other four clan chiefs to join him in rebuilding the Sacred Circle, ritual site of their ancestors. Inside the earthwork circle, he planned to erect five giant doorways, each consisting of two upright great-stones and a great-stone lintel connecting them horizontally on the top; it was my task to haul these great-stones to the Circle. With five doorways, each clan would have its own entrance to what the priests call the Other World, a world unknown to a Monument Builder like myself. The new Sacred Circle would be such an amazing sight, he said, that people would travel for miles to see it, thus increasing trade in the region. Even though Yula was the wealthiest of the chiefs of the Plain, having the richest fields and flocks and the best trade routes, he needed the others to contribute men and materials, provide food and shelter for the Monument Builders assigned to him and send gifts to the Master Builder on my home island.

He appealed to the pride, vanity, and greed of the chiefs, and then added the final argument: religion. Yula was not concerned with the old ways of the moon and death that people like Ogwyn followed. He saw himself and his own actions, rather than the spirits of the ancestors, as the cause of his clan's good fortune. Yula wanted the Monument Builders to realign the Sacred Circle with the sun, source of the clans' growing agricultural prosperity. He persuaded the priests to preach that an alignment with the sun would ensure the continuing fertility of the land and the people and thus justify the religious significance of his rebuilding scheme.

There was another reason Yula wanted to build a new monument at the Sacred Circle, a reason he confided only to me: all the work required, the stone cutting and hauling, earthworks and construction, would keep the young men of the clans too busy and too tired to indulge in feuds and raiding. He hoped that by working with men from other clans, the young would be weaned from their blood rivalries and traditional grudges, many so old no one remembered what caused them to begin with. I had already observed among my hauling crews that the power of the old rivalries, the old ways, was fading.

In my ninth spring at Avlyn, while my crews were preparing to haul the last of the fifteen doorway stones to the Sacred Circle, Fluj came to see me in Avlyn. I was surprised by his visit, because I rarely saw him. It had been six summers since Fluj completed his site preparation work at the Circle. Since then, the Master had sent him to many Monument sites throughout the world to supervise their construction or repair. He returned to the Circle three times to check on the site, but never traveled as far north as Avlyn. As soon as I saw his face, I knew something had changed.

"Myrddin, I have much to tell you, and you will have new work to do," he said. "The Master Builder is dead." I was saddened, but not surprised. The Master lived a very long time, longer than most men, more than fifty sun cycles. I had first met him over twenty sun cycles ago, and at some time during my training had come to regard him as a second father.

Before I could fully absorb the meaning of Fluj's announcement, he continued. "As you know, the Master Builder had the authority to name his successor, and he chose me. Within a week, I depart for the Boinna Valley. I want you to take over construction at the Circle. Your work hauling the stones is almost completed. You are familiar with the Monument design and what needs to be done next. And you have Yula's respect and confidence."

I realized the old Master made his choice a long time ago, by giving Fluj the most challenging assignments. Just as Fluj was the best choice to preserve and expand the secret knowledge of the Monument Builders, I was now the best choice to oversee construction of the doorways at the Sacred Circle. My mind quickly turned to the task at hand.

"But who will complete the stone hauling?" I asked. "We have one last great-stone to haul here for your doorways."

"That's up to you," he replied. "And they're *your* doorways now, not mine."

"Then I'll put Rudgawr in charge. He's worked with me from the beginning, and the men will give him their best effort." I did not tell Fluj I was relieved to rid myself of the great-stone that killed Corna or that I was happy to be staying here on Yula's Plain, near Sulis.

"Good choice. I'm sure Yula will approve. Now you and I must go to the Sacred Circle so we can talk about building the five doorways."

As we walked two days from Avlyn to the Sacred Circle, Fluj showed me a small wooden model he had made of the doorways and explained his plans in greater detail. As I listened, I realized my dead Master was correct in choosing Fluj as the new Master Builder. For many generations, we Builders knew the site of the Sacred Circle uniquely predicted the movements of both the moon and the sun, as Fluj's model so brilliantly demonstrated. He positioned all the doorways so precisely that at various seasons the sun or moon appeared to rise or set between their uprights. In all of the monuments I had seen, there was never more than one alignment with the sun or moon. Here, there were many, all in the open to be seen by the people, not hidden inside a covered tomb. Fluj had turned Yula's idea into a brilliant design, combining within it knowledge of the sun and moon that only the Monument Builders possessed.

What's more, since Yula wanted his reconstruction to honor the living, the life force of the sun, more than the dead and the cold white moon, Fluj planned to widen and thus realign the entrance to the circle, shifting it slightly so the midsummer sun would rise at the center of the entranceway. He placed the highest doorway directly opposite; since the entrance marked the midsummer sunrise, this doorway would mark the opposite, the midwinter sunset. Thus, the highest doorway in the most prominent position would honor the sun, not the moon, as Yula intended. The placement of the uprights of this doorway was crucial; Yula wanted the midwinter sun to set between them.

On either side of the highest doorway stood two more for a total of five. The uprights of each doorway would be placed very close together, no more than the width of a priest's body, and these openings would become sighting lines for the sunrises and moonrises, sunsets and moonsets. Looking through the two doorways closest to the highest doorway, a priest could track the setting moon and the rising moon. The two doorways closest to the entrance marked the midsummer sunset and the midwinter sunrise.

When we reached the Sacred Circle, Fluj pointed out to me survey stones he had placed around its perimeter. He tied ropes to them and showed me how to measure the site to determine the exact positioning of the great-stones. I had many questions for Fluj, and over the next several days he answered them all. In his design, the doorways were arranged in a shape not quite a circle nor an oval. Why? This was at the direction of the priests, Fluj said. The shape, similar to that of the Great Tomb on the River Boinna where we began our training as Monument Builders, was symbolic of a woman's womb, and so Yula's doorways, like the ancient tombs, revered the cycle of birth and death.

Although all the doorways would be very tall, four or five times as tall as a man, they were of different heights. The doorways pointed upward from the entrance, with the lowest two closest to the entrance and single tallest doorway farthest away. Why? Fluj explained he wanted to guide the eye toward the highest doorway, which was claimed by the sun, and onward toward the heavens. If there were five doorways to represent the five clans, which clan claimed the tallest one? "Ah," Fluj replied. "That's Yula's genius. He doesn't say. Lets each clan chief think the tallest one is going to be his."

We turned our attention to practical matters. My primary concern was how to keep the huge horizontal lintels of the doorways from falling off the uprights. "I hadn't thought about that much, Myrddin," Fluj said. "After all, the ancestors placed huge lintels over boulders in their tombs, and they've stayed forever."

"Yes," I answered, "but because those lintels are inside tombs, they aren't exposed to rain and lightning. And they're not mounted on great-stones more than four times as tall as a man. And what about the occasional movements of the earth? I wouldn't want a lintel to come crashing down on the priests' heads during a ritual."

"I might enjoy seeing that. These priests have far too much power, if you ask me. But I leave that problem to you, Myrddin. You have a reputation for being a smart problem solver."

"Which doorway did you plan on erecting first?" I asked. "I thought one of the two of middle heights, one of the moon doorways."

"Good thinking to do the middle height first, so you can measure the others from it. My advice is to erect one of the middle heights; then the two smallest, and then the remaining mid-height, and save the tallest for last. The tallest will be the most difficult to erect, but by that time, I'm sure you will have discovered many shortcuts and new ways, just as you did with the stone hauling. As our honored Master Builder taught us as boys, the construction and the plan are equally important. This is especially true here, Myrddin. The uprights must be placed in the exact locations we discussed. I know I can count on you to complete the work here according to plan."

I was pleased at Fluj's confidence in me and eager to get started on this new assignment. As I made preparations to leave Avlyn and move near the Sacred Circle, my only hesitation was that I wouldn't see Sulis as often. To my regret, I discovered too late that my absence gave Ogwyn the chance to indoctrinate Sulis with her backward ideas.

Gwyr

Now I am a man who has survived fifteen winters, but I was a boy when Myrddin came to live near my father's house four summers ago. Sometimes when my father Yula was busy with our farmers, and herders, and the traders who traveled through our lands, I tagged along behind Myrddin, listening and learning. Myrddin has helped me to think differently, for the ways of the Monument Builders are not the ways of the clans of the Plain.

I recall many times watching Myrddin at the Sacred Circle. If things weren't going well, if there was a problem shaping the stone, or erecting the huge uprights, or dragging the lintels to the top, Myrddin would first observe very carefully what the work crews were doing. "To solve a problem, Gwyr, you first have to know what the problem is," he told me many times. He liked to solve problems by pacing with his hands clasped behind his back, and if I spoke to him then, he didn't hear me, so absorbed was he in his thinking.

And Myrddin did devise many clever solutions. He made sure the lintels of the doorways stayed put by using the old carpenter's method of mortise and tenon, but in stone instead of wood. On what would be the very top of the uprights, he had the stone shapers level the surface except for tenons that stood up like a girl's nipples. On the underside of the lintel that would be placed over the upright, the shapers pounded out a corresponding hollow or mortise. When the lintel was placed on the uprights, the mortise and tenon locked together.

My people have been erecting stones for generations (although none so large as the ones my father ordered Myrddin to raise). First, the men dig a deep hole with one sloping side. A crew ties ropes around the great-stone and rolls it over logs until its base rests horizontally over the sloping side of the hole. Then all the strength of one hundred men is put to the test pulling the stone off the ground and up toward them, and then propping the back of the great-stone upright with tall logs. They pull and prop again and again until the stone topples into the hole and rests against the slope. The men must continue to pull until the stone stands straight, and then boys pack the pit with small boulders and chalk, tightly so that the upright will not move, and fill the hole with dirt.

We raise the lintels of the doorways in much the same way as our ancestors raised stones to roof their tombs, by building massive earthen ramps. When the lintels are in place, the ramp is taken away, basket by basket of dirt and rocks. Hundreds of strong men and boys toil at the ramps.

But Myrddin brought new ideas to our old way of doing things. He lashed together some logs through which the men pulled their ropes to lift the huge great-stones more easily. He also had the stone shapers pound the bottom of the uprights into a point, so that the men could move and turn the uprights once they were in the ground. When I asked him why the huge stones had to be put into the ground at an exact spot, not even a footstep away, he replied, "So the sun and the moon will appear between the uprights, and not a footstep away."

Myrddin shared some tricks with me. He pointed out how the stones were shaped, the uprights slightly curved and the lintels wider at the top than at the bottom. But when the lintels were raised up high and locked onto the uprights, from the ground I saw no curve. Rather, all the stones looked straight and high.

I do not understand most of the things Myrddin knows. He has studied all his life, beginning when he was a boy, even younger, he said, than I was when I first came to live near us. Even if I had studied, I know I do not have Myrddin's strength of mind. Nor do I have my father's ability to inspire and soothe with his words, to bring everyone to his way of thinking.

But I have skills of my own, strength and stamina and energy. I have youth; my father and Myrddin are both old, more than twice my age. I am lucky that in my life I have seen so many things unknown to my ancestors.

Traders bring linen, so we no longer have to wear only the skins of animals or the rough woven wool; and fine vessels for drinking and storing, not like our clumsy pots; and amber for the women, to promote fertility. I have copper for better daggers, axes and shields, and Myrddin has given my father a fine knife of a new, even stronger metal, which he calls bronze. From Myrddin's home island also comes gold, worked into the finest designs for medallions, pins, and torques.

It's not just the things we can hold in our hands that are new. My father has shared his new ways of thinking, too. He knows the sun and the hard work of our people are responsible for our wealth, not the spirits of our ancestors. The ancestors have brought us to the present, but there are many things in the present which the ancestors did not foresee. I can feel my new axes in my hands, but I cannot feel the whispers and memories of the dead.

The priests, with their old ways and ceremonies for the dead, have too much power, power that should be the Chief's. When I am Chief, the power will be mine.

* * * *

My father is dying of the bloody cough. He seems weaker each night. I sent for the medicine woman Ogwyn, to ease the pain in his chest, but I know that all her roots and herbs cannot stop the coughing. It is the same curse that brought death to my mother, and to many of our people. It is spring, the last my father will know; he cannot live through another winter.

My father always wanted to see the new monument in the Sacred Circle completed in his lifetime. Four of the doorways are standing. It is the last one, the tallest, that is causing Myrddin problems. He raised one of its uprights last autumn, but over the winter, the great-stone for the second upright cracked as it lay on the ground nearby. I don't know why; maybe from the cold, maybe from lightning, maybe from a careless workman starting a fire too close to it. Myrddin says this great-stone must be replaced. Together, Myrddin and I went to the Sacred Circle to inspect the cracked stone, and we argued.

"Myrddin, I measured this great-stone myself, using the tricks you yourself taught me. Even with the damage, it's tall enough to match its mate."

Myrddin walked around the stone, speaking slowly, as if I were a stupid child. "Yes, Gwyr," he said. "This great-stone is tall enough for what you need above ground, but remember, every great-stone needs an underground base that measures at least one-fifth of its above-ground height to support it. So this stone is not really tall enough, because it does not have the length I need for support underground. This stone will not stand for generations, as the others will."

"I don't care about generations," I shouted at him. "I only care about the present. It will take at least two sun cycles to cut, haul, and erect another great-stone to replace this one, and my father will not survive two sun cycles. For as long as I can remember, it's been his dream to see the five doorways in his lifetime. Will you deny him that, Myrddin?"

Myrddin's face flushed with anger. He swiftly strode across the distance separating us until his face was uncomfortably close to mine. For a brief moment I thought he might strike me, but I stood my ground.

"I've used all the skills of the Monument Builders to move and erect these stones faster than anyone has ever done before. You cannot say otherwise of me, Gwyr."

"I'm not talking about what you have done in the past, Myrddin," I replied, no longer shouting. "I'm thinking about the future. I want the doorways completed before winter, so my father can see them." Getting no answer from him, I added, "This is my desire, and I will be Chief when Yula is gone."

Myrddin remained silent and began pacing, as he always did when solving a problem. "I could have the stone shapers pound a knob on the bottom, to anchor the damaged stone better. But even if we did use it, Gwyr, the stone needs to settle for at least a complete sun cycle before we place the lintel on it."

Myrddin's words encouraged me, because I could see that he was at least willing to consider my request. I put forth my best appeal, as I had watched my father do many times, although I knew I was not as skillful as he.

"Myrddin, you are the best Monument Builder, some people say a magical one. But you are more than my father's builder. You are also his friend, and you know he will be dead before one sun cycle has passed. I ask you again, will you deny him his dream?" Myrddin stared at me. Although his arms hung down by his side, his fists were clenched, as if he was engaged in a great inner struggle. "It goes against all my knowledge, all my training, to do what you ask, Gwyr," he said. He began pacing again, but then suddenly stopped and faced me.

"For Yula's sake, I will do it. Now leave me, please. I have much work to do if I'm going to get this job done."

I felt proud to have won Myrddin over, and at that moment, I knew I would be a powerful chief with many great deeds. And Myrddin was true to his word. I wasn't sure that even he, with all his skill, could do what I asked, but by the ancient festival of the dead, midway between the autumn Even Day and the midwinter sunrise, the fifth and last doorway was standing.

The priests picked this festival as an auspicious time to rededicate the Sacred Circle to the sun. At sunrise, they held their ceremony inside the enclosure formed by the five stone doorways. My father and I with the other clan chiefs and their families gathered around the ancient stone in front of the tallest doorway, while the people watched from outside the earthwork circle. The priests sprinkled the wheat of the recent harvest with a powder made from the root that brings sleep, and then set it afire. They thanked the sun for the fertility of our people and our land and asked for the sun's continued blessings. As the sun rose higher in the sky, they sang and performed their holy dance. Dipping their fingers into the ashes from the burnt wheat, they painted circles on our faces. The monument was now dedicated to the sun. I could see the pride on my father's face, and he seemed strong and young again.

But as the weather turned colder, my father's coughing worsened. On the afternoon of midwinter's day, I carried Yula into the Sacred Circle. I ordered the priests to stay away, but the other chiefs were waiting: Oben, who had journeyed from the stone haulers' village of Avlyn; Ferg, who refrained from his usual mead in honor of this occasion; Dur, my father's closest friend; and Uthne, nearest in age and like a brother to me. Dur and Uthne rushed to either side of me as I lowered my father to the ground. They tried to support him, but he was too weak to stand or walk. We sat on the ground near the entrance and watched the sun set between the uprights of the tallest doorway, exactly between and not a footstep away, as Myrddin had built it.

The next day, my father died, and I became the last of my family. An older sister died as a baby before I was born. A younger brother drowned in the river. And now both my parents had crossed through the doorway into the Other World. I felt alone, but I knew I must carry on my father's work.

With my father's death, the chiefs recognized the tallest doorway as belonging to Yula's clan, because the sun set between its uprights as he lay dying. I knew that having the tallest doorway would give me greater power among the chiefs, even though I was the newest among them.

I have come to love the doorways monument as my father did. Many things change, the seasons and the weather and the length of the days. Trees shed their leaves and revive again. Babies are born, the young and the old die. But the stones remain, unchanged and unchanging, to comfort me.

Gwyr's good instincts led him to turn to the stones for solace. Gwyr could never have become Chief over all the Clans of the Plain without the great-stones that Myrddin had struggled to haul and raise as doorways. And without Yula's death, of course. Ogwyn wouldn't let us forget that Death always has a part to play.

But I must stop for now. The sun has set and I must wait for morning to continue. To light a fire may alert the Romans to my hiding place.

Maeve Haley's Blog

Modern Druids Have It Wrong
Posted August 4

I've never agreed with the modern day practitioners of the Druid religion and other assorted New Agers who flock to Stonehenge on the first day of summer to watch the sunrise over the so-called heel stone that sits outside the stone circle. I think they've got it completely backward.

Think of a compass. The direction of the summer sunrise is northeast, the exact opposite of the southwest direction of the winter sunset. The trilithons, or doorways, are oriented in the direction of the winter sunset.

The scrolls describe how Gwyr and his father watched the sun set through the tallest trilithon, or doorway, at the winter solstice, as it still does today, marking the start of the solar new year. The focal point of the monument is clearly this tallest trilithon. The two trilithons on either side of it step down; thus, the overall arrangement draws the eye to the tallest. I think Stonehenge, like Newgrange before it, was originally conceived for a winter solstice ritual.

I wonder if contemporary Druids will change their mind about this. Perhaps some ancestral memory compels them to celebrate the summer sunrise, because if you believe the scrolls, they're also celebrating Sulis' birthday.

Trilithon Mystery Solved
Posted August 4

For me, the most interesting archaeological mystery the scrolls solve has to do with the trilithons, or what the scrolls call the "doorways." They had to have been built before the stone circle, as the scrolls describe. These are massive structures, as tall as twenty-four feet above ground. It would have been impossible to erect them once the stone circle was blocking access to the site.

Three of the five trilithons are still standing because the ancient builders over-engineered, with as much as eight feet of the uprights buried below the earth. When archaeologists examined the fallen upright of the tallest trilithon, they discovered the stone was much shallower than the usual proportions. I always wondered why these ancient builders knowingly made this error; the scrolls explain that Myrddin rushed the construction to complete it before Yula's death.

"Cavemen" Didn't Build Stonehenge

Posted August 6

Andy W. posted the following comment: "Hard to believe Stone Age cavemen forty-five hundred years ago had the brains to build Stonehenge."

Our Neolithic and Bronze Age ancestors were just as smart as you, Andy W. If anything, people back then had to be more capable, both mentally and physically, to survive, even though they didn't survive for long by today's standards.

Perhaps it will help your belief to remember that the stone circle at Stonehenge was erected around the same time as the Egyptian pyramids. The Stonehenge builders were intelligent enough to invent an architectural technique called entasis, later adopted by the Classical Greeks. They tapered the huge upright stones to give the optical illusion of straightness when you look at them from the ground up,

Modern homo sapiens has been around for a hundred thousand years. So approximately 95% of all human existence took place *before* Stonehenge was built. We're living in the same, most recent 5% of human history as the Stonehenge builders. Relatively speaking, we're virtually contemporaries. Perhaps that's why Gwyr's sportsmanship or Myrddin's managerial capabilities seem familiar.

Frankly, it really annoys me when people point to space aliens or ancient astronauts to account for our glorious prehistory, when the evidence proves once again the triumph of human ingenuity.

Scroll IV

Ogwyn

The dead are always with us. The moon, her color as white as their bones, protects them as they protect us.

But if we do not perform their rituals with care, the dead can also cause great harm. I remember as a child walking the two-day journey with my parents to the Sacred Circle where they scattered the ashes of my uncle, with whom my father quarreled shortly before he died. My parents told me this act at the Sacred Circle honored my uncle and so would keep his angry spirit far away from us.

Long ago clans abandoned their village after one of their own—man, woman, or child—had died. But we cannot leave, for we have fields and animals to tend. So the old chiefs ordered the Monument Builders to erect the great tombs and stone circles that keep the dead from leaving their eternal home. When the moon is full, priests enter the tombs and carry out the bones of the dead to show the people. Thus, the people see that the dead still protect us, and the dead know they are remembered by the generations who followed. This union with the dead gives us the power to hear thoughts and speak in silence.

The dead visit me in my sleep and tell me what pleases them. In the spring I bring them freshly picked violets so the dead will bless our planting. When summer comes, I offer raspberries, the same berries that protect a woman during pregnancy, to assure an abundant harvest. The foul smelling root which brings sleep gives the dead rest in autumn. Winter demands strong medicine, the plant that grows in the branches of the oak trees, whose white berries match the white bones in the tombs. I always add herbs to ease the newly dead. Catnip protects babies who have died as well as infants who remain among the living. When a woman dies in childbirth, as my Ine did, I place on her funeral pyre the small white flowers with yellow circles, like suns fallen to earth, to honor her sacrifice. When a man is killed violently, from a fall in the quarries or a fight with another, I bring the priests the dried leaves, stems and flowers that stop bleeding among the living.

My medicines cure the living as well, their fevers, wounds that won't heal and teeth that bring pain. Just beginning her eighth summer, Sulis is already learning my cures. She can name more plants than I can count. I show her where the healing plants grow, in the marshes and meadows, forests and banks of streams. If a plant is poisonous, the one growing next to it will often contain the antidote. I tell her when each plant reaches its greatest strength for harvesting. She knows what parts of a plant will heal—its roots or stems, bark or leaves, flowers or fruit—and which will harm or even kill. I teach her to watch the animals, especially the birds, and learn from them.

Some berries we must use at once, but most sticks, bark, roots, mosses, seeds and nuts we store in our hut. We tie stems together and dry leaves and flowers. I show Sulis the many ways to prepare medicines: crushing dried leaves into powders; boiling roots to make strong, thick broths; and steeping dried flowers in a small pot of hot water. Some herbs I let sit in the hot water for a long time, and they boil themselves and turn to a drink as strong as mead. I teach her which herbs to mix together to make her medicines stronger. Sometimes we soak a cloth in a little water and a mix of healing herbs, and then place the cloth on the sick person's body; this is especially good for skin sores and also for headaches. Or we let the sick person breathe in the healing smoke from burning leaves and twigs. For babies, we wrap herbs in a small piece of cloth and tie it loosely around their necks.

It is a lot to remember, and death can come if she does not remember correctly. The stem of the rhubarb causes the bowels to move, but its leaves are poisonous. The root of the goddess plant with the big leaves and green flowers is good for all a woman's problems if it has been properly dried, but will kill if taken fresh. The mushrooms that grow on birch trees cure many different sicknesses; other mushrooms cause visions and waking dreams, but bring no cure. If the medicine is boiled too long or too much is given, it can kill. I tell her, all plants have healing power, but all have their secrets. If she is to be a medicine woman like me, she must discover these secrets, and remember them.

I fear I will join the world of the dead myself before I have taught Sulis all she needs to know, but fortunately, she learns very quickly. I think the spirit of Ine guides her, for Ine was also adept with my cures. I know Sulis visits the Shelter at the top of the hill, the stone circles where the old charnel house once stood, to be near her mother's bones. She would have been at home in that

Shelter, where the bodies of the dead were left to decay, and their bones cleaned and purified for burial, just as I was at home there.

Being so close to the dead has strengthened my powers of mind. Even now, in my old age approaching forty sun cycles, I have the mind power to hear the thoughts that are left unsaid, to know when the truth is not being told, or told only in part. This helps me greatly in matching my cures to my patients. And Sulis has a strong mind as well. She has the direct knowing; even before I teach her, she can tell me which herbs to mix for difficulty in breathing, what to drink for stomach pains or how to make a paste for wounds that aren't healing. Perhaps she is reading *my* thoughts! If she is, that foretells she will carry on the old ways. I fear others will not.

Now the clan leaders do not want their bones to be buried in the tombs of the ancestors. They no longer want us to clean off their flesh when they die and honor their bones. Instead, they are laid in the ground alone, their flesh still covering their bones, fully clothed with all their fine possessions. What good will their axes and gold arm bands do them in the Other World? Then a great chalk mound is heaped over them, forming a circle to hold them inside. When the old priest Bolc was alive, he taught the people that the moon protected the dead, but these young priests say the mound circle, the same color and shape as the moon, will protect *us* from the dead. They tell the people that we no longer need the charnel houses, because there is no need to mingle the bones of the ancestors; instead, each great leader is buried alone.

I do not understand why our clan leaders want to be separated from their ancestors, from the dead they have known. Not only are we the living separated from our dead leaders buried this way, but they are also separated from each other. What will happen to our powers of mind, when we are no longer one people living and dead, but many separate parts? I fear we have much to lose by following the young priests' teachings. Will Sulis' children and the generations that follow still hear each other's thoughts and speak in silence? When I am dead, will I be able to visit them in their sleep?

Sulis

Although my mother died in the giving of it, my father considered my birth a good omen, because I entered the world of the living—and she, the world of the dead—on the day the sun shines highest in the sky, the first day of summer.

Myrddin teaches me about the days that predict the changing seasons. Darkness and light are equal on the two even days that mark spring and fall. And winter brings the shortest day and longest night of the sun cycle. But my birth-day is the most powerful day, because it is the day with the most light.

I decided to make my own observations of the sun and marked the positions of sunrises and sunsets on the hides covering the saplings and reeds of our round hut. Myrddin was very pleased when he saw what I had done.

"Sulis, you are a clever little girl," he said. "And you're growing up to be a beauty."

But I do not want to be clever. Some people say Cwimgwily is clever, because I have taught him many tricks. I am not like a dog learning tricks from my father. Nor do I care about beauty. I want to be powerful and erect monuments upon the landscape, as he does.

My father teaches me the things he learned when he was my age. He told me about the moon cycle, only twenty-nine and a half days, much swifter than the sun cycle, I thought, until he shared the Monument Builders' secret knowledge that the entire journey of the moon across the sky takes nineteen sun cycles to complete.

"Women's cycles are moon cycles," Myrddin said. "As a boy, I didn't know that women were aligned with the moon; as a man, I often think that women are as hard to understand as the moon itself."

He told me that the Monument Builders traveled across the seas to work in many lands, just as he left his home island to come to the Plains. Each summer, he says, their Master sends messengers to all in the brotherhood, to hear reports about their new discoveries and new methods, and to share what had been reported the previous summer. "We learn from each other, what works and what does not," he said. My father is now the only Monument Builder on the Plains. After his friend Corna died when a great-stone fell on him in the quarry, Myrddin began to teach me more about the Monument Builders' ways; he had no one else to talk to about his work.

And so I learned that the best sites for monuments must have more than a clear view of the horizon. They must also radiate power, and Myrddin showed me how to measure the energy lines in the earth. He let me use his bronze measuring rod and was always pleased to see how accurate I was.

Because I was quick with numbers, Myrddin revealed to me the magic number twenty-two/seven the Monument Builders use to calculate circles. He taught me how to do the computations necessary to make small models that predict the success or failure of larger structures.

Since he left our village to work for Chief Yula at the Sacred Circle, more than a day's journey away, Myrddin comes to see me only on my birthday and the days the seasons change. But whenever Myrddin is with me, he says I ask enough questions for an entire season! He gave me his own wooden model of the doorways at the Sacred Circle.

"The tallest doorway, Sulis, captures the setting sun on the first day of winter," he explained. "The next tallest doorways, on either side, capture the moonrise and moonset. And the smallest doorways capture the winter sunrise and the summer sunset." He quizzed me again and again until he was sure I understood.

Although I want to be a Monument Builder like my father, Ogwyn wants me to be a medicine woman like her. It is easy for me to learn her cures, because I have been around Ogwyn's plants my whole life. The plants fill our hut, drying in large, round-bottomed bowls hanging from the sapling walls or stored in pots and baskets. We enjoy the plants every day, not only as medicine. Every morning, I rub my gums with water and thyme, to keep my teeth healthy, and I eat parsley to keep my breath fresh. I rub the sweet white flowers from the meadow in my hair, and I smell good. I put a few drops of sap into the water when I wash myself, and it cleans my skin. And every morning, Ogwyn and I drink water which has been boiled with pine bark; Ogwyn says this drink is responsible for her long life.

I watch the animals, as Ogwyn says, to discover new plants that heal, and new healings for plants I already know. Cwimgwily always wants to play with me in the morning, but one day he just lay on his straw bed and looked sad. I knew he was sick, so I watched as he walked into the fields and I noted what grass he ate. He peed all morning, and by afternoon he was running and jumping and bringing sticks for me to throw. I tell Ogwyn this and she is very pleased; she eats the grass herself, as a medicine woman must do, to see its effect on her own body.

"Sulis," she says, "you have discovered your first medicine."

I help Ogwyn mix her medicines, because she is very old and tired much of the time. When women come to our hut to see her—and it is usually women, sometimes with children, but rarely men—I watch and listen. Usually they want our flower-petal water, a love potion to attract a man; or the hot drink made from the two look-alike flowers with white petals and gold centers, which eases the pain that comes with their moon blood. Some want to have a baby, and we give them a powder made from the crushed flowers, leaves, and berries of the thorn tree. Others want to keep from getting pregnant, so they get a different powder made from the plant that keeps away fleas. If they are already with child and don't want to be, we give them a potion so strong it must be taken only once a day, and the pregnancy will end before seven days have passed. That is the prime concern of the women, love and pain and birth.

"Watch and learn from these foolish women, Sulis," Ogwyn tells me. "You have a strong mind. You must pick a man worthy of you, not one interested only in coupling, but a man who will accept your choosing and stay with your children."

Among our people, it is the woman who chooses a man for life mating, and if the man accepts, the priests and the people witness their pledging. But if a man does not accept and the woman is pregnant, he must provide for the child until it has seen its third winter. If he does not, the other women of the clan will shun him.

She doesn't say so, but I think Ogwyn believed Myrddin unworthy of her daughter. I think my mother wanted to mate with a Monument Builder to give life to a powerful child, and my red hair proves the blood strengthening was made in me. Myrddin did not pledge to my mother, but he accepted the local custom of providing for me and provides for me still, even though I am almost eleven. Ogwyn says he didn't want to deny himself the attentions of the clanswomen.

I go with Ogwyn when she visits the sick. At their bedsides, Ogwyn and I speak without sounds; I ask her questions silently, and she hears my thoughts and replies to me silently. As I watch Ogwyn treat the sick, I understand that it is not just her medicines that heal, but she herself. She touches the skin, to see if her patients are stiff with worry or soft with exhaustion. She hears the hesitations and the tremors in their voices and smells their breath when they answer her questions. Always, she watches their faces, especially their eyes, to know their terrors and hopes.

Before she gives them her medicine, she always says, "May this healing bring you the comfort you are seeking." Although we know the poisonous plants that bring death, she told me, "I give poisons only if the man or woman is old like me, Sulis, and only if he or she asks for death. Then I must care for them after death as well, anointing their bodies with my fragrant oils and placing white pebbles on their closed eyes and mint under their tongues."

Back in our hut, Ogwyn teaches me ways to strengthen my mind power. We burn the most powerful of our herbs and let our minds rest. Then Ogwyn says, "Imagine you are walking through a thick forest, and you reach a clearing where you see one who has died, standing and looking as if alive. Ask the dead one any question, and the answer will come." The dead one I always imagine is Ine, my mother, as she looks in my mind, although I never saw her in life. I have found the answers to many of my questions in this way.

Ogwyn teaches me the moon spell. "See yourself, Sulis, standing on a dark hill, surrounded by the light of the full moon. The moon shines on you and nothing else. The moonlight brings you calmness and energy at the same time. Feel this." Ogwyn told me she often used this moon spell herself to give her the mind power to go on with her work, despite her old age.

When the moon is full and Ogwyn sleeps, I put on the shawl that she made me from Cwimgwily's hair, go outside, and climb the hill to my Shelter. There I stand in the moonlight and absorb its power to soothe and to strengthen. The moon is the protector of the dead, yes, but the moon is also the protector of women, for women's cycles are moon cycles. Women are respected in our clan, because the moon protects them, as it does the dead. Ogwyn says our power to hear the thoughts of our clanswomen and men comes from the dead.

Everyday Ogwyn becomes more connected to the ancestors and the dead than to me. Myrddin cares nothing for our old ways; his mind is full of the work he must do today and tomorrow. But I have learned much from both Myrddin and Ogwyn, and I will use what each has taught me to find my own path.

* * * *

Ogwyn has joined her beloved dead. At forty-four sun cycles, she lived much longer than any other woman of our tribe, a tribute to her skills as a medicine woman. The pain in her belly was bad for a long time, and her body wasted to half its former size. When she could no longer rise from her straw bed, she asked me for poison. I knew I must do what I had seen her do with others seeking death. I chose the tall plant with the big green leaves and the delicate deep purple flowers. I crushed its root, shredded its leaves, and mixed them together myself. Then I put the mixture in mead which I gave her to drink.

When Ogwyn's spirit crossed into the Other World, I washed and anointed her thin body and dressed her in her cape of bark strips sewn with grass. I placed the white stones on her eyes and the mint leaves under her tongue as she taught me. Then I left her body on her bed and set our hut on fire. As I watched the flames consume my grandmother and her home, I was not sorry. Her body and her possessions had become a burden to her. Nor was I saddened by the loss of her physical presence, because I sensed her spirit was still with me. I knew she would visit me soon in my sleep.

The next day, the priests came to pray over her bones. Myrddin had the bones buried in the same tomb as my mother's, but I secretly kept one small piece of bone with me. It was the old way, the way Ogwyn would have wanted it.

I am not yet a woman, have not yet felt the pain of the moon blood. Even so, I am now medicine woman to the Clans of the Plain.

I note as I finish this scroll that my fine white robe is now soiled and dust obscures the glitter of its golden threads. I worry that the sunlight gleaming from my gold collar and bracelets may attract the attention of the Romans pursuing me, but I cannot bear to abandon my treasures under this tree for some farmer to find. But I digress.

Sulis had learned Ogwyn's lessons well to act with such courage as befits a healer. Soon her skills as a medicine woman would be put to the test for the young chief, Gwyr.

Maeve Haley's Blog

Life and Death
Posted August 7

Jim from Richmond emails: "You said that Myrddin and Gwyr seemed like contemporaries, but what about that spooky Ogwyn character? She's obsessed with death."

Ogwyn had a familiarity with death that most of us don't experience. Her generation, living under primitive conditions without modern medicine and hygiene, confronted death on a regular basis. Most people of the Stonehenge era didn't live to see their thirtieth birthday. Infections likely claimed a number of lives, women died in childbirth and infant mortality rates approached 75%. So I surmise that the populace would revere Ogwyn's and Sulis' reputations as medicine women able to stave off death.

Given that most of the population, including its leaders like Gwyr, was under thirty, I also assume the prevalence of impetuous decision-making, like Gwyr's rushing the construction of the trilithons. Your founding fathers were wise to declare a minimum age of thirty-five for any American president.

Sulis and Gwyr knew life was short, so they lived it to the fullest. Nowadays we live as if we had all the time in the world, but none of us know what will happen tomorrow.

In some parts of the world even today, however, death remains a companionable member of the family. For example, on Mexico's Day of the Dead—observed halfway between the autumnal equinox and the winter solstice, or our Halloween—grandparents, parents, and children bring picnics to cemeteries, spruce up family burial plots and enjoy the day communing with ancestors. And people today still request special access to the inner circle at Stonehenge so they can scatter the ashes of their loved one there, continuing a British tradition that's at least four or five thousand years long.

Scroll V

Gwyr

I hate to be sick. Sickness is for women and their moon cycles. Myrddin says I suffered some fevers as a child, but now, at sixteen autumns, I'm too old to be lying in my bed like a baby, hot and sweating; then cold and sweating. Yet when I try to rise, I fall back dizzy. My arms and legs ache, and my head pounds like rock hitting stone. I vomit everything I eat.

I suppose I would have met Myrddin's daughter eventually, but I would have preferred to be strong and powerful at our first encounter, not a sick man seeking her healing. Myrddin said she was a child. I've never known his powers of observation to fail him before. She is almost a woman; the summer will be her thirteenth. Enough time, I hope, for her to have learned cures from her grandmother, the great medicine woman Ogwyn. If Ogwyn were still alive, I would have sent for her all the way from their village near the stone quarry. Instead, Myrddin brought Sulis to me.

Sulis. A strange name, not like the names in my clan. When she entered my chamber with Myrddin, I saw that she didn't look like my clanswomen either, with bright red hair—like Myrddin's own, but prettier on a girl—and pale piercing eyes the color of the sky. Unlike other girls, she showed no signs of shyness nor made any effort to please me as Chief of the Clans of the Plain. Instead, she approached my bedside and proceeded with the task at hand. I knew then she was truly her father's daughter.

"What hurts you?" she asked, as her cool hand rested on my forehead. "What have you eaten? Does it stay down? Are you sleeping well or not at all?" She went on with her list of questions as she leaned over my prone body, all the time watching me intently while her fingers probed my skin. I felt her tiny breasts brush against my forearm. "Your pulse is fast," she said, but it was she, not the sickness, that caused my blood to race.

She reached into the leather pouch she carried with her and carefully selected some leaves and bark.

"What's that?" I asked.

"Dandelion leaves and bark from a willow tree," she answered. "I will make you a brew that you must drink at the times you would normally eat and before you fall asleep at night. Also drink it if you awake during the night. This will ease your fever. But your sickness is stronger than I expected. I must return to the village where I lived with Ogwyn to search among the mosses for a special mold and for a mushroom that grows on trees."

"Can't you find that here?" I asked. "Besides, I'm not sure I want to eat mold anyway."

"I don't know the plants and trees on your Plain as well," she answered. "But I will look before setting out for my village. And you *will* eat the mold if you want to live. It's of no interest to me if you live or die, but Myrddin has asked me to help you."

Myrddin, who had been silently observing her examination, quickly spoke up. "Now, Sulis, show Gwyr the respect he deserves. Forgive her, Gwyr, it's not her fault. I have spoiled her because she is my only child, and because she is so beautiful."

Sulis, busy preparing the medicine, looked up at him and smiled. A softness passed across Myrddin's usually stern face, like a ray of sunlight falling on the stones. "Well, if he doesn't take my mold, there's not much I can do to help him, Father," she said.

"I'll take your mold and this medicine, too," I said, ending the discussion.

Handing me a cup of her dandelion brew, she said, "May this healing bring you the comfort you are seeking."

I drank it down and turned to Myrddin. "I hope her old grandmother taught Sulis well."

She answered for him. "I have learned many things from both my grandmother and my father, Gwyr."

That was the first time she said my name. At the sound of it, a bulge appeared under my blanket, like a great-stone being raised. Sulis smiled again and left my bedside. Was she ignorant of the ways a man's body reveals his true thoughts, or just amused? She is a mystery to me.

But Myrddin's powers of observation had returned in full. He stared at the point where the blanket rose up.

"Her medicine must be powerful," I said to him. "I feel my energy coming back already."

Myrddin

Oh, how blind I've been! How could I have not foreseen Gwyr's erection today, when Sulis was beside his bed? How could he? She's just a child.

But then, maybe not. He's only three sun cycles older than she.

The permanence of the stones has lulled my thinking, caused me to ignore all else that is changing. But we are not stones, forever standing strong. Some days my bones ache and my mind does not see solutions as quickly as it once did. My friends Yula and Corna, men of my generation, are dead. After Corna's death, I felt even closer to Sulis, my pupil as well as my daughter. But Gwyr has made me see that she won't be a child for much longer.

I know Gwyr. He's used to getting what he wants. And so is Sulis. What a match the two of them would make!

Is he worthy of her? He's certainly the best of the lot on the Plain. But I can't bear to think of Sulis as a woman, only as my little girl. She will always be my little girl. If he hurts her in any way, I'll kill him, even if he is the Chief of the Clans.

* * * *

I had won Gwyr's confidence because Yula lived to see his five stone doorways completed. Although I had tried to explain to Gwyr that the great-stones needed more time to settle, he would have none of it, and we Monument Builders have always had to defer to the wishes of the chiefs. The doorways will stand through my lifetime and Gwyr's at least, and maybe that's enough.

Gwyr did not inherit his father's gift of persuasion, of imagining a future that the people will strive to reach. What Gwyr lacks in ideas, he makes up in enthusiasm, fearlessness, and physical prowess. As tall as I, he moves with the grace and speed of a cat. Young women admire his lean, muscular body, his long dark hair and eyes. All the young men envy the female attention he attracts, especially Uthne, the young chief of the neighboring clan. In games and sporting contests between the clans, Gwyr's passion inspires his fellow clansmen, and even his opponents do not begrudge him his victories, except perhaps for Uthne. He and Gwyr are like brothers, the best of friends and the fiercest of competitors. Gwyr will be a different kind of chief than his father was, but a good chief, too, I think.

Now Gwyr wants me to continue construction at the Sacred Circle, but unlike Yula, he does not know what he wants to build or why he wants to build it. I suggested adding a pair of stones near the bank of the earthwork circle, opposite the tallest doorway, to mark the place where he and Yula sat to watch the midwinter sun set the day before Yula died. Gwyr likes this idea, and erecting the two stones will be an easy task compared to what I have already done at the Sacred Circle. After fourteen sun cycles of building track, hauling great-stones over land and water, and raising the five huge doorways, I'm ready to rest for a while. Not as hard a taskmaster as his father, Gwyr wants to keep me around. I sense he is not as certain of himself as he pretends, because he asks my opinion on a number of things unrelated to monument building.

Don't I think we live in a new age, now that we have bronze and gold and many traders visiting the wealthy chiefs of the Plains? Don't the priests have too much power in this new age, power connected to the old ways of the dead and the moon? Why do we need the old ways? The chiefs, not the dead, create wealth for the people. That's what his father told him, he said. But what will unite the chiefs and keep the clans working together? He argues with Uthne about this. Now that Yula's doorways are completed, Uthne believes the clans should go their separate ways as before, but Gwyr disagrees. Maybe he should have listened to my advice not to rush the construction, but no, he's happy his father saw his dream completed.

On and on Gwyr says his thoughts aloud, whenever we are together. I think he realizes that to be Chief of All the Clans, he needs to give the people and their tribal leaders reasons for his actions. I listen and say little, because I do not know what to tell him. My skills and training are in building monuments; I do not know about the ways of priests and chiefs, except as they interfere with my building projects. But it does not matter to Gwyr that I say little; in fact, I don't think he notices. When he has talked himself to a conclusion, he usually thanks me for my help, although I have given no advice or comment. I enjoy Gwyr's company; I, too, miss Yula.

After Ogwyn's death, Sulis asked if she could move from Avlyn to be with me near the Sacred Circle. She wanted to practice her medicine near the place revered by her ancestors, she said, and I was her only family. I happily agreed. My dwelling, a large hut befitting a Monument Builder, had plenty of room, with mud walls, a thatched roof and a firepit on the clay floor to keep us warm and comfortable. Besides, Gwyr's reaction to her opened my eyes. I would worry if she were living alone among the rowdy young stone cutters and haulers of Avlyn; I knew them too well.

My eyes were opened to the passing of time, as well. We Builders saw death too often as we directed the dangerous work of hauling and raising great-stones. Despite our careful plans, accidents sometimes killed. But Yula's death affected me differently. That a man just a few years older than I, someone I had known most of my adult life, could be stricken with the bloody cough and die within a year made me wonder how many more midsummer sunrises I would see, how much more time I could spend with Sulis. I was so absorbed in my work, I took it for granted she would always be a little girl, and I would always be there to protect her. Now I realized neither was so.

After Sulis came to live with me, I began to appreciate the feminine influence I had been lacking since childhood. She cleaned and aired out the fur coverings on the beds, brought her plants and flowers into the hut, and laughed and smiled as I told her about my day. This same hut I had lived in for the past five sun cycles looked and sounded, tasted and smelled different with her presence. Once Gwyr asked me about her. Although he was curious about my daughter, I said little, and he did not ask again.

I am not entirely satisfied with the woman Sulis has become. Ogwyn influenced her mind too much with talk of the dead and the moon, ancient stories too strange to be believed. Why didn't she just teach Sulis about the medicines, as I taught her about building? Why add all this nonsense that you cannot see, and therefore, cannot know if it is true and real? I don't understand how Sulis, so talented at numbers and measurements—good enough to complete the Monument Builders' training, if she were a male—can at the same time believe in the superstitious religion of Ogwyn's ancestors. But it's my fault. I left her in Ogwyn's care without considering the consequences. Now the damage can't be completely undone, but I will do what I can. I'll spend time with her now, take her to the building site and divert her thoughts from the ignorant ways of her grandmother's people.

Sulis

I like living here with my father. I still gather my plants in the forests and by the river banks, in the fields, and on the hillsides. I dry and store them in Myrddin's hut now, and he doesn't seem to mind. I think he likes their exotic smells—well, most of them—and I have found some new medicines Ogwyn and I didn't have in Avlyn. Since Myrddin tells me I'm the sun's child, I search for yellow or golden flowers, powerful like the sun.

One is good to soothe the eyes. After I soak its small flowers and large sap-filled leaves, I wring a cloth out in their water and place the cloth over eyes that are pink and red with pain. Another of my golden blooms, standing tall, makes a good lotion for sores and wounds. I look for tiny yellow flowers growing close to the ground, and pick their leaves, which grow like the five fingers on my hand. Dried, ground, and brewed in a hot drink, these leaves take away all fevers. A favorite find of mine, that reminds me of a string of amber beads, eases stomach pains. I try my remedies on myself and Cwimgwily and sometimes even Myrddin. But no women come to Myrddin's hut, as they did to Ogwyn's. I think they are afraid of him. When a clan leader or someone in his family is sick, they ask Myrddin for me and I go, as I went to Gwyr. But I do not heal the people, as Ogwyn did. My father says my medicine is not for them.

Most days I accompany my father to the Sacred Circle, much smaller than I imagined it would be. There is no deep ditch like the one surrounding Avlyn, where you must walk for a long time to return to where you began and lose sight of your starting point along the way. Here, a shallow ditch surrounds a circle compact enough to be seen in one glance. It reminds me of the Shelter near my mother's grave that I often visited as a child except, of course, for the five enormous stone doorways my father has built. He boasts there is nothing else like them anywhere in the Monument Builders' world.

The first time my father took me to the Sacred Circle, so many images of my ancestors appeared in my mind, so many sensations charged through my body, so many emotions overflowed my eyes. Later I had to sit quietly to slow time, as Ogwyn taught me, and relive what happened to me there. I remembered walking up the avenue. As I crossed over the bank and stepped into the circle, I immediately felt a shock in my body, like a flash of lightning. I felt rooted in the ground, bound to the energy of the earth like one of my plants. Just as many had come before me to this spot, I knew at once that many would come after me, for generations and generations into the future, to revere this place. I felt the spirits of the dead and heard them singing, a lullaby like Ogwyn sang to me as a baby. I saw the stone uprights of the doorways turn to piles of skulls, and then turn back into stone as they caught the rays of the sun.

Back in the world of the living now, I continued walking toward the tallest doorway. The closer I got to the doorways, the bigger they seemed. My father's work—the width and thickness of the uprights, the heights to which the lintels had been raised—amazed me. I had to raise my chin up toward the sky to see the lintels lying across the tall stone uprights. I calculated that if five men stood on each other's shoulders, perhaps the man at the top could touch a lintel. This huge monument was intended to frighten, but I was not afraid. Instead, I felt the same sense of calm energy as when I imagined meeting my dead mother in the clearing of a thick forest. The dead protected me in this place built by powerful men, my father and Gwyr's father.

As I turned to exit the Sacred Circle, I noticed a strange man watching me. He was dressed in the long robe favored by the priests but with a hood covering his head. As I drew nearer, I saw his skin and hair were as white as bones, but his eyes of the weakest blue, like a cloudy sky.

"Good day to you, Sulis the medicine woman," he said, walking tentatively toward me. "I am Querke, the priest. I haven't seen you here before. Is this your first visit to the Sacred Circle?" All the while he spoke, his eyes rolled recklessly, as if their movements were beyond his control.

"Yes, it is."

"Tell me, what did you see?" he asked.

I could see the poor man was nearly blind, so I answered, "The tallest of stones, as tall of five men, forming five doorways built by my father."

"Yes, yes," he answered impatiently, "but is that all you saw? Did you see the faces of the dead?"

His question took me by surprise; how could he know what I had seen? But before I could answer, Myrddin interrupted us, putting his arm around my shoulder and almost pushing me away. "Come, Sulis, we must go home now."

"Who was that priest?" I asked my father.

"Querke. He was reared by the old priest Bolc, who died before you were born and who was a great friend of Ogwyn's. Like all priests, he's full of superstitions."

When we reached Myrddin's hut, Cwimgwily lay still near the door. An old dog now, he spent most of his days sleeping, but usually stirred and wagged his tail at my approach. When I leaned down to pet him, I saw that he had died. Cwimgwily had been my companion for as long as I could remember, and I took his death as another sign my childhood was ending.

That night, the bleeding started. Ogwyn came to me in a dream and instructed me to take the medicine made from the two flowers with white petals and gold centers. "Now you are a woman, able to have a child, but you must wait," she reminded me, a warning she had given me many times when she was still among the living. "Your body is like my Ine's, your mother. Wait a few sun cycles, Sulis, before allowing yourself to conceive." I did not tell my father this, nor did I tell him what I sensed at his doorways.

Every time I went with Myrddin to the Sacred Circle, I asked him questions about the doorways. How did he get the huge great-stones from Avlyn all the way here? Why were the stones shaped the way they were, curving slightly? How did he raise the huge uprights and secure the lintels to them?

Myrddin answered all my questions in great detail. Even more than he loved his work, he loved telling me about it. All the Monument Builders' stone circles, he said, were designed to capture and even predict the movements of the sun and the moon, and he revealed to me the secret relationships between his doorways and these movements. In our hut I found the small wooden models he had made of the doorways, three different models until he achieved the correct placement. Myrddin took the final model to the Circle and showed me how its measurements were repeated, in a much larger scale, in the doorways before me. My father paced out the measurements of the Sacred Circle, instructing me how to find its exact center using the four stones that served as corners of a rectangle. He taught me how to calculate the distance around the Circle by measuring the length of a straight line drawn through its center and computing with the secret numbers of the Monument Builders, twenty-two and seven.

I helped him with the measurements and computations for the two new siting stones Gwyr wanted him to erect just inside the circle, facing the tallest doorway. It was I who added to his model, showing in wood miniatures the exact position of the new stones. I listened as he instructed the haulers and stone finishers, and I observed the workers following my model to dig the holes for the siting stones. And all the while I was watching the work crews, Gwyr was watching me.

I heard Gwyr's thoughts. He remembered when I came to heal him, and he recognized my power as medicine woman, not unlike his power as Chief of the Clans. He saw how Myrddin instructed me, and this intrigued him. He would have approached me before now, except Myrddin was always with me.

The silly girls in the nearby village gossiped about Gwyr, some bragging they had slept with him and others plotting to. They reminded me of the foolish women who came to Ogwyn looking for love potions and pregnancy herbs. I did not let them know that I, too, admired Gwyr's rugged face, with his strong chin and deep set eyes. I longed to touch his thick, dark hair, pushed back from his high forehead, and hold his tall, lean and muscular body close. But I knew his secret thoughts, the ones he did not speak, and how he disdained the women who pursued him, even though he never rejected their favors.

One day when Myrddin was away in Avlyn visiting his foreman Rudgawr, Gwyr came to our hut. "I want to talk to Myrddin about some ideas for building more monuments," he said. When I told him Myrddin wasn't there, a fact I suspected he already knew, he said, "Would you like to walk with me to the Sacred Circle?"

"Yes, Gwyr, if you promise to tell me about your plans for building."

Gwyr said little as we set out for the Circle, as did I. I was content to breathe the musky scent of his body beside me and feel a breeze from his strides wash over me. When the five stone doorways came into view, we stopped to admire them. "See how they dominate the Plain," he said. "Like a mountain ruling the landscape, like the powerful clans they represent."

"My father has told me how you insisted he raise the tallest doorway in Chief Yula's lifetime," I replied, gazing up at his handsome profile. "I'm sure that was a great comfort to your father."

"Yes. It gave him strength as he left this life." His voice cracked and he cleared his throat. He took a few steps forward, and then turned to face me. "And I will be forever grateful to your father for his achievement."

We continued our stroll through the burial mounds that surround the Sacred Circle. Gwyr didn't speak, but I could hear his thoughts of his father. I let his memories flow until I finally broke our silence.

"The people say your father was a great man, Gwyr, to convince the clan chiefs to build these doorways."

"My father saw the future. He knew the clans must stop their feuding and work together. He told them this new monument would attract more traders to our Plains and bring more wealth for the chiefs, and what he predicted has come true. He also told me keeping young men from the different clans working together builds bonds of friendship as well as monuments."

By then we had reached the avenue that leads to the Sacred Circle. We did not enter into it. Only participants in ceremonies were permitted to enter the Circle, with the exception of the workers (including my father and me as his assistant) erecting Gwyr's two new siting stones. But this was neither a ritual day nor a work day.

We paused a short distance from the entrance to the Circle and allowed our eyes to take in the sight of all the massive stones. The five huge doorways surrounded the ancient standing stone that marked the place of honor. Four low stones at the edge of the circle defined the rectangle from which Myrddin taught me to locate the Circle's exact center. Gwyr's new siting stones lay nearby awaiting their permanent posts.

"It looks like you and Myrddin will have both my new stones in place by this time next summer," he said.

I nodded. "Then what will you do to continue Chief Yula's work?" I asked.

"I want to keep building," he replied without hesitation. His chin thrust forward and his words poured out rapidly. "Without a new monument to build, I fear each chief will think only of his own territory, and the clans will revert to feuding against each other. But building something will keep the clans united under my leadership, and then there will be no doubt that I am truly Chief over All the Clans of the Plain, as my father was."

"Yes, but *what* will you build next?"

He kicked a pebble on the ground, and for a moment he seemed like a little boy. "I don't know," he said.

"My father says Chief Yula's doorways inspire because they have meaning beyond mere stonework," I said. "The doorways represent the five clans and their placement rededicates the Sacred Circle to the Sun."

"Yes, that's so, Sulis. Five clans, five doorways, but it's still one monument. So I think the doorways also show us what can be accomplished if the clans work together as one clan. I believe in the power of the united clans."

I grabbed his arm to emphasize what I was about to say. "Then whatever you build, Gwyr, must have that meaning, your meaning."

Gwyr seemed encouraged, whether by my words or my touch, I couldn't determine. As we walked back to Myrddin's hut, he told me how he planned to win the support of all the tribal chiefs by his own deeds, and not just the memory of his father's. He spoke kindly of Chief Dur, a gentle farmer and Yula's dear friend, who had become like an uncle. He asked if I knew Oben, chief of my village of Avlyn, a great herdsman who had more children, by many different women, than sheep. He admired Chief Ferg, a sharp trader, even when he had drunk too much mead, which was often the case. But he seemed fondest of Chief Uthne, just a few sun cycles older and a frequent companion.

I smiled and nodded as he described the fine gold daggers and bronze axes the traders were offering, marveled as he boasted of the races and fighting contests he had won and laughed as he regaled me with stories about deer hunting with Uthne, who sometimes treated him like a much younger brother. But all the time my deep thoughts were elsewhere. I was thinking of the new monument I wanted to build.

The story of Sulis' romance with Gwyr inspired many fantasies and dreams among us young lads. Oh, how we desired Sulis and envied Gwyr! Speaking of Gwyr always recalls my own athletic youth. Even at thirty years of age, I am still a swift runner and have eluded the advancing soldiers thus far. But for now I must find a safe place to sleep.

Maeve Haley's Blog

Sulis' Medicines

Posted August 9

Several of you have posted questions about Sulis' use of plants in healing. "Is this just a fairy tale or could she really cure diseases?" John from London asks.

Primitive medicine men and women in places like Belize and the Amazon continue to amaze contemporary scientists with their plant-based remedies and herbal cures. Cancer researchers, in particular, have funded promising studies in these areas. So yes, I believe her medicines were effective in many instances.

Sulis treats Gwyr with willow bark tea, which would contain the same ingredient as aspirin; a mushroom that grows on trees, probably birch fungus, a known antibiotic, and a special mold that is likely a type of penicillin. She gives Ogwyn the root of a plant with deep purple flowers; my guess: belladonna, a powerful poison.

I'm most struck, however, by the healer's techniques Sulis learned from Ogwyn: touching the sick person's skin, smelling her breath, saying the healing prayer. Was that more powerful than the impersonal, high tech medicine we experience today?

The Magic Number

Posted August 11

Scott Austin posts: "What's the significance of the 22/7 number the Scrolls refer to?"

Haven't you guessed? Twenty-two divided by seven is 3.14, a close approximation of pi, which, as you may recall from your schoolboy geometry, is the ratio between the circumference and diameter of any circle. This was truly a key ratio for the Monument Builders to have discovered, for it allowed them to do relatively accurate calculations for any circular structure.

Pi was known to the ancient Egyptians, who were building their pyramids at around the same time the Stonehenge trilithons and stone circle were being erected, so it's not inconceivable that Myrddin and Sulis were aware of its use. An artifact from ancient Ireland also seems to confirm that the Druids there were in on the secret.

If you go to the National Museum of Archaeology on Kildare Street in Dublin, you'll see on display on gold crescent-shaped collar called a lunula from the Early Bronze Age, a period that may overlap with the Stonehenge builders. Seven semicircular rings of gold make up the collar, which is clasped by two large golden discs, each with eleven circles around its circumference, for a total of twenty-two. Thus, the design of this magnificent piece of jewelry indicates the Irish Druids revered the secret 22/7 number.

Scroll VI

Gwyr

I must have her. I long to touch her high breasts and discover if the hair between her legs also matches the color of the setting sun. I think of all the ways I want to make her cry out in passion. So why do I hesitate to pull her close to me and kiss her? Because Sulis is not like the other girls I have known, soft, yes, but powerful, too. I see how Myrddin has taught her, as he once taught me, maybe more than me, because his daughter shares his inclination for building.

Perhaps I hesitate because of Myrddin. What would he do if I slept with Sulis? Myrddin acts differently with her, not the stern taskmaster, never able to order her about as he orders the work crews. What kind of girl can overwhelm even Myrddin's cool authority? When I asked him about her, he told me little except that she was born on the day the sun stays longest in the sky. I took it as a good omen for a future lifemate.

I need Sulis, but I cannot choose her. By the custom of our people, the woman chooses her lifemate. But I can use all my advantages to convince her. It shouldn't be difficult. Who else could she choose more desirable than me?

I thought surely I would have her after the feast I gave on the Even Day, the day before the clans begin digging and clearing the fields for planting. In the two sun cycles since my father died, I have held many feasts for all the chiefs and their families, to strengthen my friendships and alliances with them. This time, I invited Myrddin as well, so he could talk about future building at the Sacred Circle. And Sulis.

She looked especially beautiful that day, her long red hair tied behind her neck, and at her waist, a woven belt with a gold buckle she said Myrddin bought for her last birth-day commemoration, her fourteenth. What a strange notion, I thought, remembering the day of your birth. Behind her right ear she wore an herbal sprig of small white flowers with a sweet smell, and I wondered how she got flowers to bloom even before the planting had started. I saw the chiefs looking at her, Dur and Oben with admiration, Ferg with curiosity, and my friend Uthne with lust, and that made me want her all the more. When I asked her to sit next to me, they nodded their approval. Uthne poked me in the side with his elbow and leered at me with a dirty grin. Myrddin frowned, but said nothing.

My cooks had outdone themselves. They served trout and snails to begin, followed by a roast pig with apples, my favorite, and berries and hazel nuts. The drinks flowed faster than the food, mead made from my honey, and beer from my barley, and an occasional drink of rainwater. Musicians played their pipes and drums and sang a bawdy song about a farmer planting his seeds for a crop of sons and daughters.

Then Chief Ferg showed us the bronze axe he had recently traded with some traveling smiths for a supply of flint. The other chiefs marveled at the spiral design cut into its wooden handle and praised its gleaming axe head so much, I knew I had to show something equally as fine. From my pouch I extracted a huge piece of amber, tied with a leather string to make a necklace, which I had traded for some time ago. I had been saving it for the woman who would become my lifemate. Its size impressed the chiefs, and their wives and daughters admired its color and the insects trapped within.

Just as I was thinking that its golden glow reminded me of Sulis, she said, "See how these insects appear still to live, as if they had survived death itself." What a remarkable thing to say, and everyone, men and women, even Myrddin, looked at her in awe. On impulse, I put the necklace around her neck. "Now it looks more mysterious and beautiful, with you as its keeper." She smiled and cupped the amber in her hand, and I imagined it was I she was fondling.

"Amber has healing energy; a good gift for a medicine woman," she said. Uthne guffawed and I heard a few whispers around the table, but I didn't care. I thought she would give the amber back to me, but she wore it through the rest of the feast.

As the sun was setting and my guests began to depart, I hoped Sulis would stay with me. Surely, she knew I favored her. But she went with Myrddin, taking my amber with her and leaving me to Uthne's ridicule.

"Either Ferg needs to give you some lessons in trading, or I need to give you some lessons in women."

I resented Uthne's implication that he knew far more than me; after all, he was just a few sun cycles older. I ignored his remark, but Uthne wouldn't stop.

"You gave her your amber, but got nothing in return, not even a tiny kiss! If I had given her the amber, I would have expected at least one night in her bed," he said.

"I'll win her soon enough," I replied. "Can't you see she favors me?"

Uthne snorted. "Women are known to change their minds," he said. "Time will tell whom she favors."

The next day, I saw Sulis at the Circle as usual, helping Myrddin. She was wearing the amber pendant, as she did every time I saw her after that. I longed to find her alone, but others were always around, haulers and pounders, cooks bringing food for the workers and, of course, Myrddin.

Finally, there came a day when Myrddin wasn't at the Circle. I asked Rudgawr where he was.

"He's off to Avlyn for the day, to look at some new stone he wants to cut. But I saw Sulis head off to the forest, probably to get some plants and bark for her medicines."

I hadn't asked him about Sulis' whereabouts. Why did he tell me? Had my longing for her taken on a visible shape of its own that all could see, or an odor that all could smell?

At last my opportunity had arrived, and I set off to the forest to find her. I spotted her in the distance, bending over to pick some yellow flower, her hair falling forward and hiding her face. When she saw me approaching, she rose to her full height and looked straight at me, waiting. She was wearing the amber pendant. I walked toward her, wondering what to say. I didn't have to say a word. She kissed me full on the mouth, soft and sweet but confident, too.

After the kissing went on for some time, I moved to unfasten her dress, and for the second time that day, she surprised me. She stopped me. Confused, I tried again, but I couldn't mistake her refusal. I could have overpowered her easily, but she is Myrddin's daughter. She hugged me and stroked my hair.

"We will meet again soon," she said. "Now I must gather my flowers, while they still hold the morning dew."

And we did meet again, many times, in the forest, at Myrddin's hut when he was occupied at the Circle, and at my compound, after the cook and housekeeper left for the day. A remarkable girl, different from any other I have known, far beyond the way I imagined she would be when I used to stroke myself in frustration! Her breasts are neither too small nor too large, a perfect mouthful. And yes, the hair between her legs matches the color of the blazing sun. She tells me exactly where and how to touch her, and I don't mind following her directions, because it arouses her to even greater passion. She teases and touches me, strokes me, puts me into her mouth. I have never had another girl do that before. She seems unafraid, and yet, she will not let me inside her. I would burst with longing, but she relieves me with her hands and her tongue. But it's not enough. I will never get enough of Sulis. How will she ever choose me, if she won't let me make love to her?

Sulis

I think about Gwyr all the time. As I make Myrddin his hot herb brew in the morning, I imagine I am making it for Gwyr. When I gather my roots, leaves and flowers, I make sure to take for myself those that give a sweet smell and those that prevent pregnancy. When I see Gwyr at the Circle, I can't look at him, for fear I will kiss him then and there, in front of everybody. And in my bed at night, I remember his touch and fall asleep dreaming of our bodies together.

He hasn't taken me yet. As I learned from observing all those foolish women who consulted Ogwyn, only an unwise woman lets a man have his way too soon. Three full moons have passed since Gwyr gave me this amber. I don't know how much longer I can wait. He is the only man I have ever wanted or will ever want.

During our secret times together, I feel so many strong emotions overwhelming my body, just as I did when I first stepped into the Sacred Circle. Connected to Ine and Ogwyn and the women who came before them, I see glimpses of the children who will come after me, my children with Gwyr. The Gwyr I have come to know, strong and full of life energy and wanting the best for his people, does not think and plan like Myrddin, but most of the time, his instincts serve him well. But like his father, Gwyr dismisses the old ways, the ways I learned from Ogwyn.

I told Myrddin I wanted Gwyr to be with us for my fifteenth birth-day commemoration. "What is your interest in Gwyr, Sulis, and what is his interest in you?" Myrddin asked me.

"If it has anything to do with building your precious monuments, I'll let you know." I replied. Myrddin's eyes opened wide and his eyebrows rose up, but he asked nothing more.

Later, I pondered Myrddin's question. Because I can hear Gwyr's thoughts, I know he intended the amber pendant for his lifemate, and he has not asked me to return it. He does not see me as just another girl for sex, but as someone different and powerful, like his new gold, bronze, and amber objects. As Myrddin's daughter, I will bring sought-after new blood into the clans. The chiefs respect Myrddin; they will approve.

When I thought about my interest in Gwyr, I realized I had not answered Myrddin truthfully, for my interest *is* tied to his monuments. Once Gwyr is my lifemate (and I know he will accept my choosing), I will convince him to let me build the monument I have been thinking of, the one that honors both the old ways and the new, the moon and the sun, the dead and the living, woman and man. If Gwyr were not so handsome and virile, would I still choose his power, so I can build my monument? I'm glad I don't have to answer that, not even to myself, for I am a Monument Builder's daughter.

* * * *

Myrddin presented me with my own bronze measuring rod for my fifteenth birth-day, a true honor, since only Monument Builders, not even the chiefs, carry the rods. Gwyr gave me a fine bow and a sheath of arrows, and promised to teach me how to shoot. He also brought me a puppy, one of a litter that Cwimgwily fathered.

"I think it was that siring that killed your dog, Sulis," Myrddin said. "I wouldn't have believed he had it in him."

The three of us ate the special meal I prepared, pheasant cooked with raspberries, bread, and wild cherries. I gave the puppy some goat's milk to drink. Myrddin talked more than usual—about presents he had given me on my previous birth-days and about Gwyr's parents, Yula and Aya. This was his way of telling us he approved of our being together.

That night I slept in Gwyr's bed. Not much sleep, really, but at least I rested between the times we made love. I bled, of course, and that frightened him a little. He thought he'd hurt me. He'd never been with a true virgin before.

I explained, "The first time, with blood, is for the moon goddess."

It made me feel powerful, the power of a woman, to have him galloping inside me. I trusted him completely and let my body melt into his until I saw stars lighting up the night, rising and setting like a thousand suns.

We spent more time alone together after that. I liked to try different ways to make love, and Gwyr was eager to explore with me.

"Sulis," he told me, "you are a clever girl in more ways than one, I see. Medicines and monuments and love, too."

I found it harder to be apart from him for more than one night, but believed I needed to deny him occasionally, to keep his interest.

"You're torturing that boy, Sulis," Myrddin said one evening after supper, "and yourself, too. Why don't you just choose him? You must see by now that he is yours for the asking."

"Oh, so now you are an expert on love, are you, Father?"

"No, but I know more about men than you do, Sulis. And remember, I've known Gwyr since he was a baby."

I knew at once my father was right, so I went to Gwyr immediately and found him just within his dwelling. He lifted me up and carried me to his bed. We kissed and stroked until I had to have him. I lowered myself onto him, and moved slowly up and down and around. Then quickly, both of us came together, spent and happy.

I rolled myself off him and turned to look at his glowing face, relaxed like a child's. "Gwyr, I choose you for my lifemate." As was his way, he didn't stop to think, not for an eye-blink.

"I will be your lifemate, Sulis, and what a life we will have together. As soon as everyone's awake in the morning, we'll arrange for the pledging ceremony."

And so before the second full moon after my fifteenth birth-day, I pledged to Gwyr in the Sacred Circle. I wore a dress of fine linen tied with the belt with the gold buckle Myrddin had given me and the amber pendant from Gwyr. I carried the two symbols of my family, the measuring rod from Myrddin and a bouquet of my most powerful plants, all with yellow flowers. All could see Gwyr looked like a powerful chief. Two gold discs, representing the sun, were sewn onto his soft wool tunic, and a new copper dagger encased in fine leather hung from his belt.

We stood before the chief's stone, in front of the tallest doorway that was now acknowledged to represent Gwyr's clan, and faced those who were gathered to witness our pledging: the chiefs and their families, Myrddin, and by special invitation in recognition of the many times he had helped my father, Rudgawr, now bent and lame from his life of stone hauling. The strange-looking Querke and a few other priests witnessed the ceremony, too. Gwyr wasn't happy about that, but I convinced him we needed their presence. Many of the people—haulers, stone pounders, cooks, cleaners, diggers, child minders, farmers, animal keepers—stood outside the circle to watch and listen.

As the sun rose, Gwyr said, "I, Gwyr, Chief of the Clans of the Plains, son of the great chief Yula and his lifemate Aya, pledge to you, Sulis, to be your lifemate, to father your children, to care for you and take your side always."

And I replied, "I, Sulis, daughter of the Monument Builder Myrddin and the medicine woman Ine, pledge to you, Gwyr, to be your lifemate, to bear your children, to care for you and take your side always."

The priests sang their hymn to the sun, asking for fertility for our union and for our lands. They poured the blood of a deer onto the ground, sprinkled flax seeds onto it, and covered it all with dirt. Our pledging was thus accepted by the earth, and her animals and plants, as well as by the sun.

We left the Sacred Circle and returned to Gwyr's compound for a celebration. As we watched performances by flute players, drummers, dancers and singers, each chief approached us in turn to offer congratulations.

"You will be a great chief, as great as your father, with Sulis' help," Chief Dur told Gwyr. Uthne, Gwyr's best friend, was the last to greet us. "So you have finally won her, after all," he said to a beaming Gwyr. Turning to me, he continued, "Gwyr has made the best match for himself." Although he was smiling, I detected jealousy in his thoughts.

The chiefs and families toasted us many times in a great show of the unity of the Plains clans. Finally, Myrddin, who had drunk every toast, rose to speak. "A wish for my beautiful child, Sulis, for a long and happy life with Gwyr, who just may be worthy of her." The crowd laughed and drank, but I saw tears escaping my father's eyes.

I hugged him and whispered, "Don't worry, Myrddin. You haven't lost a daughter. You've gained another Monument Builder."

Gwyr declared a three-day holiday with food and drink for all, chiefs and workers alike. The clans gathered in the cleared field near the Sacred Circle for days filled with games and nights filled with love. Men and boys competed in Gwyr's favorite contests of skill and strength: races, wrestling, stone tossing and lifting, archery and axe-throwing. He awarded the winners prizes of meat, cloth, and leather. Each day when the sun began to set, I arranged for music and dancing, and couples wandered away to enjoy each other. Many matches took place during our pledging holiday.

All the clansmen and women could see Gwyr was a true chief, proud and in charge. He no longer seemed a youth, perhaps because, aroused by the contests, I made sure to fill his nights with lovemaking games of my own.

Enjoy whatever happiness life sends your way, dear reader, as Gwyr and Sulis did, but you must always be mindful of those who envy your good fortune. I learned this as a judge, after hearing much envious testimony from feuding nobles. Our lovers' bliss hid the animosity lurking, which I shall next reveal.

But now I hear the shouts of a soldier. The Romans are too close. I must retreat toward the sea.

Maeve Haley's Blog

A Few Thoughts on the Druids
Posted August 13

Mr. Nigel Moore has got himself a lot of publicity recently by stating, "No reputable archaeologist would imply that the Druids built Stonehenge. That's a folk tale, at best."

As a reputable archaeologist, I know history first records the Druids about two millennia, plus or minus a century or two, *after* the stone circle was erected. However, I do believe there's a strong likelihood that the *descendants* of the Stonehenge builders may have been Druids.

Julius Caesar, who wrote the first account of the Druids, noted their tradition of committing to memory "a great number of verses" during a long course of training. The Monument Builders had such an extensive training period, and perhaps memorizing the stories of the great builders Myrddin and Sulis inspired their oral tradition.

Like the Monument Builders, Druids were just about the only educated people of their day. Although the popular stereotype depicts Druids as pagan priests, they in fact comprised all the learned professions, such as judge (like Oisin, our scribe), historians, poets, physicians, teachers and advisers to kings. And like Myrddin/Merlin, the Druids were regarded by the populace as wizards and magicians.

Unlike the Catholicism in which I was schooled, Druid rituals were often led by women, powerful druidesses like Brigit in ancient Ireland.

Perhaps those "folk tales" Mr. Moore derides contain an element of truth.

Scroll VII

Gwyr

I crept quietly through the field following Uthne and his dog. Suddenly the dog stopped, and I immediately readied myself to shoot. As the dog leapt forward, a pheasant hastily fled, and I followed its flight and released my arrow. The bird fell, my arrow stuck in its breast, and I raced the dog to retrieve it. Uthne reached my side just as I was stuffing my prize into a leather pouch.

Uthne and I have hunted together for as long as I can remember. His father, also a chief like mine, died from an attack by a boar. When Uthne's older brother took over as chief, the boy, Uthne, was left in the care of his mother, who spoiled him and indulged his every whim. Following his brother's death from drowning—he was drunk at the time—Uthne became chief of his clan. He has been my best friend all my life.

"Another lucky shot, Gwyr," he said. "You always were lucky, but now since you're lifemated to Sulis, you seem to be luckier than usual."

What Uthne said was true. After our pledging celebration, the clans experienced a bountiful harvest. The hunting had also begun well, with three deer brought to my compound yesterday. The people will be well fed this winter and on into the spring, and Sulis shall have a new cloak and shoes from the hides.

Living with Sulis has made me calmer and more sure of myself. Every morning she mixes the hairy leaves of an herb with small purple flowers with some water, and she has me rinse my mouth with it. In the evening, she serves me a special brew, one that Ogwyn taught her to make and which she believes accounted for her grandmother's long life. She's got Myrddin drinking it, too. She makes it from mashed berries, the blue and red ones that grow on evergreen trees. I haven't felt a day's sickness, not a cough or a headache, since I started drinking it.

Since Sulis chose me as her lifemate, Chiefs Oben, Dur, and Ferg, who were loyal to my father, have come to realize that I am more than Yula's son, no longer a boy, but a man. Only Uthne still thinks of me as a younger brother. He taunts me for teaching Sulis to shoot with a bow and arrow instead of spending more days hunting with him.

"Must be all your time in bed with Sulis that makes you so lucky," Uthne continued. "The village girls have all given up on you. Oh, remember the times we had with them, you and I?" He nudged me as if he were expecting me to tell him all about my intimacies with Sulis. I don't know why he thought I would betray her trust by revealing what is only for us to know. Uthne has always been curious about Sulis. After the feast when she took my amber necklace, he pestered me unmercifully about her. It can't be an unsatisfied urge that spurs his interest, because Uthne always has plenty of women willing to lie with him. Perhaps he lusts after Sulis himself.

I didn't answer his question, but that didn't stop Uthne. "So when are we going to see Sulis' belly grow?" he asked. "With all the copulating you two have been doing, she's sure to be pregnant by now."

I smiled. "I like having her all to myself, with no babies to distract her," I replied.

"But don't you want a son to tell of your great deeds after you're gone, as you are doing for your father and I for mine?"

"Of course. Eventually."

"Maybe there is something wrong with your seed. Perhaps it's not potent enough to make a baby," Uthne teased.

Infuriated, I pushed him hard, and taken off guard, he lost his balance and fell to the ground. I threw myself down on him and we wrestled like boys. Uthne's dog circled around us, barking at us as if we were puppies.

Finally Uthne said, "I take it back. Let me up, Gwyr."

We stood up and dusted the dirt from our clothing. It annoyed me that I felt childish, like the little brother Uthne still considered me. "You forget Sulis is a medicine woman," I told him. "She mixes for herself the herbs that keep babies from forming. There will be plenty of time for children later."

Uthne didn't reply, but his dog ended our quarrel by taking off in search of another bird, and we followed silently on our hunt.

Sulis

Life at Gwyr's compound has given me much to think about. Unlike the quiet life I had with Myrddin or Ogwyn, now I am surrounded by people and activity. Farmers and herders deliver their crops and animals to the cook and her helpers, who feed us and all the workers here. Artisans and metalworkers craft fine daggers. Leather tanners sew cloaks and shoes for the winter. Occasionally traders arrive, bringing with them not only polished stones and finely woven cloths, but also stories from their mysterious lands bordered by vast seas.

Like the other chiefs, Gwyr makes all decisions regarding the grazing fields, farmlands, forests, and rivers within his territory. He determines who can hunt or fish and when, which fields will be planted and which will lay fallow, and who will work on the Monument Builder's crews. As chief, he receives as tribute one of every six animals or fish caught or baskets harvested. The people count out five portions with the fingers on one hand, and then set aside one for the chief.

Like Yula before him, whenever monument building was underway at the Sacred Circle, Gwyr also received the same measure of tribute from the other chiefs, one for every six they collected. In return Gwyr provided food, housing, and clothing to the haulers, stonecutters, and their families. As Chief of All the Clans, Yula also acted as judge, settling disputes between people from different clans without favoring his own relatives or showing bias against men and women from outside his clan. Gwyr wants to assume his father's role as Chief of All the Clans, but to do so, monument building must resume.

Gwyr had a small hut built just for my plants, and I spend my mornings there, drying the leaves and grinding them into fine powders, chopping roots, and for my strongest medicines, steeping the herbs in grain water. One morning, Lena, a cook's helper, came to see me. She burned her forearm while removing a pot from the fire and was crying from the pain. "You are not from our clan, but you are the lifemate of our chief," she said, "so I ask you to heal me."

"I am medicine woman to all the clans of the Plain," I told her. I felt a kinship with them all; a healer cannot refuse to give care. I sat her down and gently washed her arm. I mixed some sap with water and cooling herbs and applied it to her skin. From that day, Gwyr's clanswomen came to my hut seeking cures and potions.

I still go to the Sacred Circle almost every afternoon, whenever Myrddin is there, and Myrddin eats with us at the compound most evenings. Gwyr likes his company and relies on his advice as well as mine. Myrddin sees that we are happy; it surprises him a little, I think, because he never accepted a lifemate himself.

Every night, we make love. I like the feel of our bodies united, of his power surging into me and my spirit into him. He is eager for lovemaking and as skilled at it as he is in his games and contests, with his athlete's body and lover's heart. There is no other man I will ever want, for none can surpass my lifemate. And he tells me I am the most desirable woman he has known and that he can't get his fill of me. I know this is true, for he often awakens me during the night to make love again.

I make sure to take the herbs as Ogwyn told me in my dream the night the moon bleeding started, because my body is like my mother's and I must wait to have a child. I thought Gwyr might object to the waiting. Certainly other men, like Chief Uthne, believe a man must father a child to prove his manhood. I know Uthne has taunted Gwyr because I am not pregnant. Gwyr just laughs and challenges Uthne to beat him in hunting or games, which Uthne has been unable to do since they were boys, even though he is older. Many, like Chief Oben, think lots of children cause the land to be fertile. Gwyr dismisses this belief as part of the old ways. It is the sun god, he says, who brings prosperity to our fields and herds. He doesn't mind waiting a few sun cycles for children, because he can have me all to himself in the meantime.

Although Gwyr has lived his entire life knowing he would one day become a chief, I am just beginning to understand their ways. Seeing all the chiefs at our wedding feast made me wonder. Are we one clan or five? It cannot be only the monument building and the settling of disputes that binds the chiefs to Gwyr, that binds the people to each other. If that were so, why do I feel a bond with all the people, from powerful chiefs to servants like Lena? We do not see the traders who pass through our lands as one of us, as one of our people, yet they have bodies and minds like us, they are not animals. What makes us different from them? What defines our people?

Gwyr, with his new ornaments made of copper and gold, thinks wealth and power unite a people. If that is so, why were the ancestors one in the old days when there was no gold and no worship of the golden sun? So united were the ancestors that they could speak without words and hear each other's thoughts. Now, only a few like me have that power. Gwyr may disregard the old ways, but many of the people—and I suspect, at least some of the chiefs, like Oben—fear what will happen if the dead are not appeased. The old ways are like that part of the upright stones of my father's doorways, buried deep under the earth. You cannot see the buried part of the stone, but without it, the upright would soon fall. Without our beliefs and our commitment to each other as a people, our clans will fall. I know this to be true in the deepest part of myself.

Despite my lifemate's worship of the sun god, I cherish the old ways of the moon, for the moon protects women as well as the dead. I fear what will become of women in future generations if the moon is not honored. Will we still be allowed the plants that protect our bodies from too many births? Will we still choose our lifemates, or will men choose us? Will men still be required to acknowledge and feed their infant children?

To destroy the old moon rituals for the sake of the new rites of the sun would be like destroying my heart. But to reject the new and preserve the old unchanged would be like destroying my mind. Just as my heart and my mind reside in one body, the old ways and the new ways can both reside in our people. I must find a way to make it so. And for that, I will need to make the priests my allies, especially the one they call Querke.

He stood out among the priests at our pledging ceremony, with his white skin and hair. He always wore a long robe with a hood to protect his ghostly skin from the sun. His strange appearance caused many to fear him and others to believe he possessed magical powers and could see into the future. No woman would go to his bed. They were afraid of giving birth to another pale stranger like Querke. I have heard this from some of the women seeking my cures, who say Querke was abandoned as an infant. The priest Bolc, of whom Ogwyn often spoke with great admiration, took him in and schooled him in the old ways, so it was natural for him to take on priestly duties when Bolc died. Besides, I have observed he seems to enjoy the company of his priestly companions, one youth in particular.

Myrddin has no regard for priests, whose requirements make the Monument Builders' work more difficult. And Gwyr resents their power over the people; a power he believes should belong to him alone. But I have an opinion different from either my father or my lifemate. I intend to take the power of the priests for myself.

One morning, as I was working in my plant hut, Querke, accompanied by his youthful companion, approached. He is a frail man, no taller than I, older than Gwyr but not as old as my father. Querke entered while the youth remained outside.

"Good morning, Sulis the medicine woman," he said. "Do you remember me? I am Querke the priest." He said this with all seriousness, as if I or anyone could possibly fail to recognize him.

"Yes, Querke, I do," I replied. "What brings you to my healing place?"

He undraped his hood and bowed his head before me. I immediately saw a bright red spot at the top of his head, where his fine white hair no longer grew. "I'm afraid I fell asleep in the sun," he said. He smiled like a child caught in mischief, and I instantly knew I could trust him. I had no fear of him whatsoever.

"I can make a kind of milk that will ease the sting of the burn," I told him. It was the same medicine I prepared for Lena. "It won't take me long."

While I mixed the sap and herbs, Querke stooped to examine my pots of leaves, roots, and stems. At first, I thought he was smelling them, but when he held a root up so close to his eyes that the root touched his forehead, I remembered his pale eyes barely allowed him to see. When I handed him a small bowl with the milk, he lifted it to his mouth. "No, don't drink it," I said. "Dab a little on the burn, and repeat again before you go to bed, and in the morning when you wake." Again, he gave me that childlike smile.

"But since you thirst, I will give you a special drink, one that assured my grandmother's long life." I poured us both a cup of Ogwyn's brew from a supply I stored in my hut.

"You are very kind," he said. "As a child, I heard many stories about the great medicine woman, Ogwyn. I am honored you share her brew with me." So he knew Ogwyn was my grandmother. I immediately realized he had come here to appraise my character, but I, too, had intentions. We drank in a comfortable silence while I waited for the brew to loosen his tongue

"The people say you are a good lifemate for their chief," he began.

"And what do the priests say?" I replied.

Querke did not answer me directly. Instead, he said, "Chief Gwyr acknowledges the power of the sun god, on whom we all depend for life."

"I am under the sun's protection because I was born on the day the sun rises highest in the sky," I said. "But as a woman I also acknowledge the power of the moon, as my grandmother taught me."

He stared at me as hard as he could with his blinking eyes. I read his thoughts and knew he was trying to decide if I could be trusted, if he could say what he truly believed. But Ogwyn's brew overcame his fear and finally he spoke. "I conduct the sun rituals for Chief Gwyr, but like you, I, too, have been brought up in the old ways of the moon."

"Your skin makes you the moon's creature, not the sun's," I told him.

"That is an astute observation," he said as he rose to leave. "We must talk again."

"Yes, I'm sure we will," I replied.

As I watched him walk away, I realized that the youth was his guide, gently steering him by the elbow away from obstacles in his path he couldn't see. I was determined to steer him, too, toward a new religious path that embraced both the moon goddess and the sun god.

Sulis' determination to preserve the old ways, taught to her in childhood by the great medicine woman Ogwyn, inspires me to complete this history. I still have plenty of ink made from crushed oak apples and iron, and quills taken from a swan's tail feathers. I pray I can finish writing before the Romans find me, so that our way of life will not be completely forgotten.

But remember, dear reader, Sulis was not just Ogwyn's granddaughter, she was also Myrddin's daughter, and monument building was never far from her thoughts.

Maeve Haley's Blog

What's in a Name?

Online chat

August 15

Sean from Seattle asks, "Why don't the scrolls ever mention the name 'Stonehenge'?"

Maeve replies: The word Stonehenge wasn't coined until the Middle Ages, or about a millennium or so after this scroll was written.

Sean: "Sounds like another piece of evidence that the scrolls are genuine."

Maeve: Good point, but the radiocarbon dating has already established the date of the scrolls as first century AD.

Sean: "Does that mean the story they tell is true?"

Maeve: Some things in the scrolls can never be proved, because corroborating evidence just does not exist. If it ever did exist, it's been lost or destroyed in the forty-five or so centuries that have passed since Stonehenge was built. For example, I can't prove there was a fraternity of Monument Builders, although it makes sense to think there was. Nor can we prove that Sulis herself was a real person. Yet her story is told in an authenticated document written twenty-five hundred years after her death, and that document is as valuable as an original of the *Iliad* or the *Odyssey*, epic stories told for generations by illiterate bards to illiterate listeners. They weren't written down until centuries later either.

Nigel Moore from England joins the discussion: "Just because they've been put to writing doesn't mean we believe that Ulysses walked the earth and encountered the Sirens and Cyclops."

Maeve: Dr. Moore, we're honored to have your input.

Moore: "Like the legend of King Arthur, this story probably has some element of truth in it, and a lot of fanciful imagination as well."

Maeve: Couldn't you say the same of the Bible? How do we know that Joseph had a coat of many colors? Who can verify that Jesus multiplied the loaves and fishes? Some things we take on faith.

Moore: "Miss Haley, as an archaeologist, I'm a scientist, not a rabbi or priest."

Maeve: Yes, but think how much the Bible has influenced and continues to influence the entire course of Western civilization. What if we had these scrolls two thousand years ago? How would our society be different?

Maria from Washington, D.C., joins the discussion: "I think women would have gotten a lot more credit."

Scroll VIII

Gwyr

My darling Sulis is perfect in every way but one: she is always nagging me about what I want to build. Her questions frustrate me because I know I must start building soon if I am to be acknowledged as Chief of All the Clans of the Plain. As my father taught me, monument building attracts the favor of the sun by drawing traders and the wealth they bring and unites the clans by giving all a common achievement. Without another monument to build, the clans will go back to feuding and raiding. I know this, yet I cannot imagine a new monument as powerful as my father's: the five doorways, one for each clan.

"Your father's doorways honor the sun, but whatever you build must also honor the old ways, the ways of the moon and the ancestors," Sulis told me one evening, as we were preparing to go to sleep.

"I don't care about the old ways," I replied. "I don't believe in them, and I won't honor them." I stripped off my cloak and lay down in our bed, waiting for her to join me.

Instead, she stood over me.

"But I do care about them," she replied. "And so do many of the people and priests as well."

I watched her undress, a sight that always stirred me. "Well, when I am Chief of All the Clans of the Plain, I will order the priests to worship the sun and forget their moon rituals." I reached for her, but she turned away.

"That would be foolish, Gwyr. You can order the priests' ceremonies, but you cannot change their deepest beliefs. Or mine." She slipped into bed beside me. "Perhaps you should talk to Querke."

"I don't know why you bother with him, Sulis. If he weren't an albino, people would be talking about the amount of time you spend with him."

She glared at me. "Don't be ridiculous," she said. "Can't you see that it's better to make the priests our allies, rather than our enemies?"

"The priests keep the clans separate by devising different rituals for every clan," I replied. "I have no use for priests."

"Yes, you do," she argued, "and it's time you realized that without their support, you won't succeed in uniting the clans." And with that, she closed her eyes and turned her back to me, without giving me so much as a goodnight kiss. She soon fell asleep, leaving me to toss and turn.

The next morning, she continued the discussion I wanted to avoid.

"People at Avlyn and here at your compound come to me for healing, mostly women, it's true, but I hear their concerns. They need their rituals to console them. Perhaps because I had no siblings, no mother and a father who was often absent when I lived with Ogwyn, the people became part of my family. How can you be Chief of All the Clans of the Plain if you do not understand your people? You are isolated here in your compound and with the chiefs."

I didn't know how to defend myself against her accusations, but she didn't wait for my response.

"You and my father are alike in some ways, Gwyr. You both think building a new monument is enough to win power, but it is not. If you want to truly unite the clans, you need to give the people rituals and beliefs all clans can share."

I had an answer for her. "If I do as you suggest, the priests will still have too much power, power that should be mine as Chief of All the Clans." I thought that would settle the argument, but once again, Sulis surprised me.

"Then let me help you take their power," she said. "I can be your priestess as well as your lifemate."

I wasn't sure what she would do as a priestess, but I liked the idea of usurping the power of the priests. Is it so strange for the Chief's lifemate to be his priestess? It has not been done before, but there has not been a woman like Sulis before. Would the people accept her as their priestess? All acknowledge Sulis' powers as a medicine woman, and she is the daughter of Myrddin, whom many see as magical for moving the great-stones. It would not be so long a step from medicine woman and magician's daughter to priestess of all the united clans that I will rule as Chief.

Sulis

While I was rummaging through some baskets and pots in my planting hut, I came upon Myrddin's old wooden model of the five doorways he had given me to remind me of the many Monument Builders' secrets. I picked it up to take a closer look. The siting stones I added to it for my father were still intact.

I must have been lost in memories because Querke startled me, so quietly had he and his young guide approached. "Your father is a magical Monument Builder, Sulis," the priest said. "It's a shame he never fathered a son to carry on his work."

I felt my face flush in anger. His daughter can also carry on his work, I wanted to reply, but mistrust held me back. Instead, I turned away from Querke to hide my emotion and carefully placed the model on a shelf.

"The doorways are a glorious tribute to the sun," Querke continued. "But you and I, dear Sulis, still revere the moon's power as well."

"Yes," I said. I gave him some more healing milk to protect his pale skin, but this time I did not offer him any of Ogwyn's brew, so annoyed was I by his remarks.

My conversation with Querke lingered in my mind all day as I was caring for my plants. I *am* a Monument Builder, I told myself, and I can design a new monument for Gwyr that does preserve the old ways of the moon. Although eager to build, Gwyr had no specific structure in mind. He was a man of action, not of ideas, and I'd learned it was no use talking to him about the old ways and new ways. But I knew if I could *show* him a model, he would react, and I could use Myrddin's model as the basis of my new design.

But what would I design? I turned the model, looked at it from all sides, and tried to imagine where a new monument would fit. But there simply wasn't enough room to erect another impressive structure inside the Sacred Circle. And that's where I had to build Gwyr's monument, because all the important rituals of the clans had always taken place there. No other location would do.

It seemed an unsolvable dilemma, to erect a monument at a place where there was no space for a monument. But I remembered a mind trick Myrddin taught me. When he encountered a particularly difficult problem, he let his mind rest, and the answer would suddenly appear before him. He told me that was how he got the idea to move the great-stones on the river instead of over land, as they had always been transported. And so I let my mind rest. Every day when I tended my plants, I gazed at the model, but no solution came to me.

Then one night I dreamed I was a child again and walking uphill, as I often did, toward the Shelter, where I sat in the center of its little circle of stones all around me. When I awoke, I had my answer. I would build a circle of stones around the entire site of the Sacred Circle, but my circle would be made of great-stones as tall as my father's doorways. Enclosing the five doorways with a circle of stones would signify to the people that the clans were now united within this sacred boundary, a design that would appeal to Gwyr, I knew. But I also wanted my design to honor the old ways of the moon, and I wasn't sure how to achieve this.

I pondered this problem throughout the day and, as if reading my thoughts, Querke appeared at the door of my planting hut again. "Did you hear the thunderstorms last night, Sulis? My master Bolc used to say that in thunder we hear the voices of the dead returning to instruct the living."

"Ogwyn told me the same when I was a child," I replied. Querke nodded.

"What was Ogwyn trying to tell you last night?" he asked. Not awaiting my reply, he turned and went on his way.

Querke's question puzzled me. Ogwyn always told me the old ways of the moon protected us, just as the circle of stones I envisioned would protect the five doorways. So the circle would be a moon circle, I thought, and then another idea came to me, so fast I thought lightning flashed outside. I would build my circle with thirty great stones, twenty-nine wide uprights and one narrower stone, to honor the twenty-nine-and-a-half day cycle of the moon.

With this moon circle of stones, the people would be able to mark the days of the moon's cycle, and remember its power to protect both the dead and women who bring new life into the world. Just as my father placed lintels upon the uprights to form his doorways, I would place lintels all around my circle of stones, connecting them all, as the days and the people are connected. I would thus unite, in stone that would stand forever, the male sun and the female moon, as Gwyr and I were united. My stone circle would glorify the old ways of the moon to remember the dead and the new ways of the sun to inspire the living. When I next saw Querke, I thanked him for his question.

"Dear Sulis," he said, "I am only reminding you what Ogwyn would tell you if she were still among the living. And in honor of my master Bolc, I will do whatever you ask to help you restore the rightful place of the moon at the Sacred Circle."

From then on, I knew I could count on Querke to justify my plans to his fellow priests, and I trusted him implicitly.

Now that I had a vision of what I wanted to build, I took my father's model and added to it a circle of wooden sticks topped by a circle of lintels. When I visited my father at the Sacred Circle, I discreetly checked my measurements and lines of sight, and then came back to the hut and adjusted my model. I soon saw the circle of stones I wanted to build could also be used to track the movements of the sun and moon, as my father's doorways did, but more easily and accurately.

As I worked with the model, I vowed to build my stone circle strongly, so that generations and generations to come would see it and remember us, and in this way, Gwyr and I would defeat even death. To sustain Gwyr's new monument, I planned to create a new ritual, one that also conquered death. With the help of the moon and my powers as a woman, I would show Gwyr what he must build.

Gwyr

My darling Sulis surprised me once more. My Monument Builder's daughter had been thinking about what I needed to build to become Chief of All the Clans of the Plain. She showed me a wooden model for another monument at the Sacred Circle. Her very clever design enclosed my father's doorways in a protective circle of great-stones, capped by lintels all around. I had never seen anything like it.

"Where did you get this idea?" I asked.

"I got the idea from you, Gwyr, the day we first walked around the Sacred Circle together, and you told me of your vision of the power of the united clans."

She explained to me the meaning of her model, how her stone circle honored the moon and showed the old ways protecting the new. But what I really liked about her design was that all the clans were united within the circle. That was my thinking, and she had captured it in stone. For some reason, she did not want to show the model to Myrddin right away. She feared he wouldn't approve, although I couldn't see why.

Sulis wants the Sacred Circle to be the holy gathering place for *all* the people of all the clans during the rituals for the herd, the planting, and the harvest. But when I become Chief of All the Clans, I will permit only chiefs, priests and those who do heroic deeds for the people to enter my inner circle of stones. The rest can watch from outside the stones, on the earthwork. Our clansmen and women will thus strive to do more, to please me, so they can join my inner circle.

Sulis said I needed new rituals and beliefs to go along with my new monument. I had no interest in the animal sacrifices, the chanting and dancing, the prayers and such things that occupy the priests, but I finally admitted to myself Sulis was right. Her years of living with Ogwyn in Chief Oben's village made her close to the hopes and fears of the people, and as a woman, she felt their emotions more strongly than I. With her as my priestess, creating new rituals for my new inner circle, the power the priests now have will be surrendered to me.

My circle of stones, with its ring of lintels, will dominate the landscape even more than my father's doorways do now and proclaim the wealth and power of the Clans of the Plains to all who enter our territory. By building this great circle, Sulis and I will be remembered for generations to come. And Myrddin, too, I suppose. I have convinced her to let me show him her model.

Sulis' model for a circle of stones preserved the Monument Builders secret geometry of mathematical ratios and proportions that we teach today. What would our priesthood be without such knowledge handed down for generations?

We also honor the balding Querke by cutting patterns into our hair; mine identifies me as a judge. I cannot allow these traditions and our history to disappear. I must write more quickly.

Maeve Haley's Blog

Stonehenge as a Calendar
Posted August 17

Perhaps of all the modern conveniences we take for granted, none is so ubiquitous as the calendar. We forget that rulers and priests, emperors and popes struggled over centuries to perfect a method for tracking time.

The calendar familiar to most of us is based on the sun, but not all calendars are. The Hebrew and Muslim calendars follow the lunar cycle.

Although Stonehenge had many uses and significances, some of which will remain forever mysterious to us modern humans, it's easy to see that the placement of the stones marked the movements of the sun and the moon, and thus served the function of a calendar. The thirty stone uprights in Sulis' circle (half are still standing, but archaeologists have found evidence for the rest) count off the days of a month. Repeat the count twelve times: then count the five trilithons (or doorways), and you have three hundred sixty-five, the number of days in a year.

Some have speculated that the Neolithic people went to all that effort moving giant stones so they could track the sun and moon to know when to plant their crops. They must be city folks. Having grown up in rural Ireland, I know farmers can tell when to plant by the condition of the soil or even the movements of birds and animals.

The reason our ancient ancestors required a calendar was to set accurate dates for their religious rituals, a practice continued even today. Easter falls on the Sunday following the first full moon after the vernal equinox. That's why Easter isn't on the same date very year, because it's based on a lunar occurrence, not a solar one. Christmas, on the other hand, does occur on the same date year after year. The early Christians chose the December 25 date to replace the pagan winter solstice celebration, a solar event.

Women in Neolithic Times
Posted August 18

Clair from Pittsburgh posts: "As a feminist, I was pleased to see a woman play a major role in this history, but also surprised. I thought women in ancient times would be much less liberated than Sulis seems to be."

Depends on what you mean by ancient. My Celtic and Pictish female ancestors were about as liberated as you can get sexually and financially. They kept their own names and property after marriage; in fact, inheritances were matrilineal (some say because they could never be sure who the father was).

The Neolithic/Early Bronze Age period was probably a relatively peaceful and stable time. Archaeologists haven't found evidence of fortifications, for example. It was also a time when art was valued, as we see in the stone carvings and even the designs on pottery shards. It doesn't appear to be a macho society.

Women likely weren't second class citizens in 2500 BC because their fertility was too highly valued, first, because the mortality rate was so high, but also ritually, as a link to the fertility of the land and crops in this new agricultural age. Besides, Sulis had a lot of power backing her: Gwyr, the local chief; her father, probably the most educated guy around; and Ogwyn's revered and perhaps feared reputation as a healer.

There are thousands of these ancient tombs and stone circles throughout the UK, Ireland, and France, and I've studied most of them. None have a circular rim like the one that connects the huge uprights of Stonehenge or its beautiful proportions and careful shaping of the stones. It's not such a huge leap of faith for me, as it is for Nigel Moore, to believe Stonehenge was designed by a woman.

Throughout history, there have always been exceptional men and women, geniuses who rise above the prevailing prejudices by the sheer strength of their intelligence. I'd have to put Sulis in that category.

Scroll IX

Myrddin

At this point in my life, having survived forty winters, I expected no more surprises. I have seen the winter sun rise into the Great Tomb on the Boinna River, and the winter sun set between the uprights of the highest doorway at the Sacred Circle. I have known wise men, strong and persevering, as well as stupid, lazy men. I have made love to many women, and sometimes found the plain women to be better lovers than the beautiful. I have moved giant stones and raised them, more quickly than anyone had done before. And I am a father as well. If there were to be any surprises left for me, I should have known they would come from my daughter.

When Gwyr came to my hut with the wooden model of the new monument he wanted to build, I was stunned. The model showed the five stone doorways I had struggled to erect now enclosed by a circle of thirty huge great-stones, as high as the doorways, and all joined at the top by a ring of stone lintels. I could see in my mind how powerful this monument would appear at its full size, dominating the Plain even more than the doorways do now.

For a moment, I wondered if Gwyr hired another Monument Builder nearer his age, as I had been with Yula. Who was this young builder who would design such a wonderful monument? But when he handed me the model to examine more closely, I recognized my own handiwork. Of course, it had to be Sulis who had taken my old model of the five doorways and added to it. I wondered why she hadn't shown me her design as she was working on it.

I taught her well. As I turned her model and peered at it from different viewpoints, I saw her measurements were perfect—the relationships of the stone circle to the doorways and the center of the site, the distances between the stone uprights of the circle, the curvature of the lintels. I noted with a smile that although there were thirty columns in the circle, one column was only half as wide as the others—twenty-nine and half columns, to count the days from one full moon to the next. She always was a very clever girl!

Her columns were evenly spaced, except at the northeast, where there was a wider space to allow viewing of the midsummer sunrise from inside the circle. In fact, at no place did her new circle of stones obstruct the sighting lines from the doorways; if anything, the space between the great-stones of her circle made the direction of the sunrises and sunsets, moonrises and moonsets, even more obvious. And where the uprights in her stone circle did block the view from the doorways, there was no meaningful sun or moon position to see, at any time of the year. She also managed to leave undisturbed the four stones that marked the late Master Builder's rectangle; like Fluj's doorways, her design improved on the Master's discovery.

I also saw the hidden meaning in her work Gwyr couldn't have seen, how she used the Monument Builders' secret numbers for the sun and the moon in her measurements, and how she linked these heavenly bodies with our sacred geometry. Her model was unlike any created before, perhaps because no women had designed monuments before. Hers lacked nothing to make it complete or more beautiful.

"Sulis made this, didn't she?" I said, more a statement than a question.

"You've discovered it. I told her you would know," Gwyr replied. His eyes brightened and his face was alive with the enthusiasm I had so often observed in him as a boy. "Well, what do you think?"

"It would be a wonderful monument, Gwyr. But..." I hesitated, not wanting to dampen his spirits.

"What, Myrddin? Speak freely. Sulis isn't here. You can tell me your true thoughts."

"Gwyr, almost twenty sun cycles ago I began hauling stones for your father's doorways," I began. "The purpose of his building was to re-align the Sacred Circle with the sun, protectors of the chiefs and their wealth. That has been done. It is the new way. And this stone circle would take us right back to the old ways of the moon and people like Ogwyn. I fear Sulis has been too much influenced by her grandmother. To go back to the old way now..."

But before I could finish, Gwyr interrupted me.

"Why not have the moon as well as the sun, Myrddin? Both appear in the sky. Besides, many of the people still find comfort in the ways of the moon. Yes, Sulis' design does combine the old and the new"—he took the model from me and traced its circle of lintels with his hand—"but what I really like about it is that the stone circle unites the five doorways, and so makes the five clans one. That is my vision, which will live forever in her circle of stones."

Gwyr was not a deep thinker, but he was a good leader of men because he was able to focus his mind on a single big idea. Although I could see her monument said and did many things, he saw only his idea of a united people, and I knew Sulis used this to convince him. I realized why she hadn't wanted to show me the model before now. She needed to make sure Gwyr was on her side first.

"So you've already promised her you would have it built."

"Yes," he said, sitting himself and the model down on a bench.

I stood over him and my voice rose in frustration. "Will you always give in to my daughter, Gwyr?" I expected him to deny this, but instead he rose and looked me right in the eyes.

"Perhaps giving in to Sulis is one of the many valuable things I've learned from you, Myrddin."

I couldn't deny his charge. I reached down for the model and held it between us.

"Well, can I at least lower the height of the stone circle, so that the doorways are higher? That makes the sun more prominent than the moon, so you'll be honoring your father's vision. And you'll still have your own vision, too, with the clans' doorways united within the circle."

Gwyr listened intently, but said nothing. I guessed he was wondering how Sulis would react to my suggestion, so I said, "You can tell Sulis that lowering the height of the uprights in her circle shows the predominance of the new ways of the sun, but the old ways are still there, encircling and protecting the new. That should satisfy her."

"Yes, I like that idea, Myrddin. I'll ask her to change the model, and make the uprights of the circle shorter than the lowest of the doorways." I couldn't help smiling at the look of excitement that reappeared in his eyes. "Then I'll show the model to the other chiefs." He paused for only a breath before proceeding with his thoughts. "When they see it, I know they will want to build it, for no people anywhere have a monument like this. But they'll ask me how many sun cycles it will take to complete. What shall I tell them?"

"Let me think out loud and compare this job to your father's doorways. It took thirteen sun cycles, nine to haul the fifteen stones for the doorways, and another four to raise them, and that was rushing it, as you know." Gwyr smiled, perhaps at the memory of our past arguments about raising the damaged great-stone, but said nothing, so I continued with my analysis.

"My hauling techniques have greatly improved, and the stones for this new circle are smaller. But there are many more of them—thirty for the uprights and another thirty for the ring of lintels—and I can no longer rely on Rudgawr's help. He is too infirm. Raising all these lintels will be a tough job, but we won't have to raise them as high as the doorways. And since the lintels are all connected, we may not have to build as many earthen ramps, or maybe we can reuse parts of the ramps as we proceed around the circle raising stones. The crews will certainly get faster as they gain experience placing the uprights into the ground and raising the lintels. And remember, we'll need a full year for all the uprights to settle."

I paused to reflect on all these considerations. Finally, I said, "My conclusion is we'd need almost as much time, ten to twelve sun cycles to build it."

Gwyr listened without comment, but he surprised me when he said, "In twelve sun cycles, I'll be almost the age my father was when he died. So we better get started right away."

I thought to myself, I am too old and too tired to build a monument of this magnitude. So I hope my darling daughter realizes what she's about to take on.

Sulis

For the past three sun cycles, young men from all five clans have been hauling stones for my circle. Gwyr asked each of the chiefs to designate a foreman to direct the workers and keep their spirits high, as Rudgawr did for my father. I was grateful for their help. Myrddin, at more than forty sun cycles of age, could no longer exert himself with the stamina he mustered for Yula, so I also accompanied my father to the work sites.

Myrddin and I took turns going to oversee the stone haulers, about once each crescent moon, to see that they were following our instructions correctly and to make improvements where we could. The men did not object, because I often assisted Myrddin before I pledged to Gwyr, and as Gwyr's lifemate, I already had their respect. Besides, as their medicine woman, I was concerned with the well-being of the stone haulers. Their risky work caused too many crushed limbs and broken bones, even deaths. So I sought out ways to make their work safer, as well as easier.

I once observed at the Sacred Circle how my father erected a tall wooden structure consisting of two logs slanted toward each other and joined by a crossbar toward the top. His crew was then able to raise a great-stone by pulling on a rope draped over the crossbar, its opposite end tied to the stone.

I had similar structures built on hilltops over which the great-stones were moved. As I had seen my father do, I instructed the haulers to tie ropes around a great-stone and lift the rope over the crossbar of my wooden structure. But instead of pulling on that rope, I had the crew tie it to a second great-stone on the opposite side of the hill. When they pushed the downhill stone with logs, the stone going uphill was pulled by the weight of the downhill stone. At the same time, the weight of the stone going uphill kept the downhill stone from moving too quickly. When the haulers realized how my method made one stone help the other, they began to acknowledge me as a Monument Builder in my own right and not just my father's assistant.

I next organized the haulers into three crews: one to move the great-stones from the fields near Avlyn to the river, a second to float the stones along the river, and another to transport them from the river to the Sacred Circle. By concentrating on one part of the journey rather than taking the stone along the entire journey, the men gained skill more quickly. Not only did fewer injuries occur, but the stone hauling went faster.

Because I wanted my monument to be beautiful as well as powerful, I alone directed the stone shapers and finishers at a site near the Sacred Circle where the great-stones were held awaiting construction. Men had always done this hard pounding work, but shaping the circle of lintels called for more precision and challenged all their skills. To guide them in shaping the curvature of the lintels, I cut a pattern from deer hide. I then assigned women and girls to the fine finishing work needed to smooth the rough surfaces of the lintels and uprights. Fearing the men would object to sharing their work with women, I asked Querke to intervene with the chiefs. Querke told them that because the stone circle would honor the moon, women needed to take part in its construction to assure the moon's full protection.

Only Uthne saw fit to disapprove of my participation in monument building. Once when I was directing the stone finishers, Uthne approached. "I always thought you were a woman of many talents, Sulis." He leered at me and looked me up and down when he said this, to make sure I understood his meaning. Although furious, I didn't reply, because I didn't want to cause trouble between Gwyr and his friend.

But even Uthne had to agree when the chiefs told Gwyr there had never been such excitement on the Plains, because the people sensed we were building a sacred monument to inspire future generations. I was not yet ready to think of future generations from my own body and used all my skill as a medicine woman to keep from conceiving. Only once in these past four autumns since I pledged to Gwyr did I suspect I was with child, and I knew how to cure that. The time was not right. I had too much work to do, not just monument building but also devising a new religion so Gwyr could take for himself the power held by the priests.

As Gwyr's priestess, I would honor Yula's belief that the sun god brings us food and life. As Myrddin taught me many years ago, Yula's five doorways proclaimed the sun's dominance because three of them, including the tallest, were directed to the sun. Yula worshipped the manly sun, the giver of life to his crops, the source of his wealth and power. Gwyr carried on his father's beliefs by wearing a gold breastplate and a copper dagger to draw the powers of the shining sun to him.

But I wanted to make the people see again what our ancestors always knew, that the moon, not the sun, protects us in death. For when men die, even chiefs like Yula, the sun god cannot bring life again to their bodies, but can only cause them to rot. My circle of twenty-nine and a half stones, to count the days of the moon, will restore the balance between sun and moon at the Sacred Circle, and the balance between the male power and female power in the lives of the people.

I will teach a new belief, which came to me in a dream, that the moon can revive the spirits of the dead. The moon protects women as well as the dead, for is not the moon's cycle the same as the cycle of women? When a woman's body generates life, I believe the moon puts the spirits of the dead into her womb. In this way, the spirit of a man or a woman can live on, in a new lifetime in a new body. Inside the Circle, I will observe a new holy day this spring, even while the construction continues, to show the people how a spirit can come back to life.

Here is my ritual: I will give a man a womb-shaped cup, so he can regenerate himself. Into this cup, he will put the fluids of his body, his spit, sweat, urine and sperm, along with life-giving water, and then offer this cup up to the moon. He will spill the cup on the ground as a symbol he will come back to this place after death. He will observe this ritual every spring, the time of rebirth of the plants, on the first full moon after the Even Day. When he dies, his cup will be buried with him, as the womb that will regenerate his spirit into an infant born on the Plains.

The clanswomen will not need cups, for they can regenerate themselves from their own wombs. Instead, they will bring to the ritual on the first full moon after the Even Day their blood of the moon, to spill on the ground and so assure the rebirth.

When the chiefs come to realize that they can live again, but perhaps in another clan, each will see how foolish it is to think only of his clan. They will begin to see beyond the boundary stones that mark their lands and recognize they are united as one people within my circle of stones. Now the five doorways are separate, as the clans are, but when my circle is completed and encloses the doorways, the clans will become one under Gwyr, whose power will be strengthened by my new rituals.

Soon Gwyr must ask the chiefs for more men, a fifth crew to begin raising the uprights. As the clansmen begin to see my stone circle take shape before their eyes, they will want to work harder to see it completed.

We hold to Sulis' great discovery even today, because we have observed the spirits of our dead leaders returning to live on in future generations. By practicing the proper rituals, we will conquer death and live again in a new time. I pray my spirit is reborn to see the day the Romans will be overcome.

I am too exhausted to continue writing. Tomorrow I must complete this story.

Maeve Haley's Blog

Reincarnation
Posted August 21

Sulis' preaching of reincarnation no doubt held a strong appeal in a death-obsessed culture. Furthermore, as Caesar noted, the Druids also believed in reincarnation, "that souls do not die but pass after death from one body to another," the primary tenet promulgated by Sulis.

The cups Sulis used in her reincarnation rituals provide another answer to a longstanding debate. Archaeologists have uncovered many of these beakers and speculated about them endlessly. Most think the objects represent a new, more refined civilization brought by newcomers to the Salisbury Plain, whom they dubbed the Beaker People. A lot of silly academic chatter about differences in skull size between the alleged newcomers and the natives has since been largely discredited, but the physical evidence of the cups themselves still tantalizes.

Stonehenge Astronomy
Posted August 23

Today I want to share an online chat with Cecilia R., who posted the following: "I don't understand the emphasis in the scrolls on the summer sunrise or winter sunset. What would be different from summer to winter? Doesn't the sun rise in the east and set in the west no matter what the season?"

Not exactly. Depending on the time of year, the sunrise ranges from northeast to southeast, and the sunset, from northwest to southwest. The sun rises directly in the east—and sets directly in the west—only at the spring and fall equinoxes. To the people of Stonehenge, it appeared as if the sun was moving across the sky. Now we know, of course, that it's the earth that's moving, orbiting around the sun and rotating on its own axis.

Cecilia R. replied, "Okay, but what's so special about the Stonehenge sunrises?"

There are four stone markers at Stonehenge called the Station Stones that define a rectangle. Myrddin referred to them as the Master Builder's great achievement. The short sides of the rectangle mark the sunrises and sunsets, and the long sides mark the extreme risings and settings of the moon. What's interesting is that this ninety-degree relationship between the extreme lunar and solar positions exists *only* at the latitude of Stonehenge.

Perhaps the Monument Builders discovered that relationship by accident, but I don't think so. I've seen hundreds of Neolithic and Early Bronze Age tombs and circles, and most are situated on high mountains or overlook rocky coastlines, lakes or rivers. The Salisbury Plain, where Stonehenge stands, boasts no such spectacular natural scenery. I conclude that the site for Stonehenge was chosen precisely for its sun-moon relationship.

Cecilia R. wonders, "Why does the ninety-degrees matter?"

This ninety-degree relationship makes it easier for the cognoscente like Sulis to predict eclipses. Today most people don't pay them attention at all, but four thousand or so years ago, an eclipse was a major event, whose power could make good omens better or bad ones more threatening. To know in advance when an eclipse was coming would be a powerful piece of intelligence.

Scroll X

Gwyr

Uthne handed over the fish we had caught to his cook, and then poured us each a cup of mead. "A good day, Gwyr," he said, raising his cup. "Just like when we were boys."

We had spent the morning fishing. On the way back from the river, Uthne recalled the friendship of our fathers, and the many times we fished and hunted together. "Remember when you thought you had caught a big fish, and it turned out to be a tree branch entangled on your line?" he asked. I had to laugh at the memory.

It had been a while since I visited Uthne's hut. Although large and filled with his many possessions—furs and knives, bows and arrows, pots of mead and bowls of nuts—his lodgings lacked the comfort of mine and Sulis'. There was no order to the arrangement of goods, no flowers to bring a soothing scent, no one singing as she worked. Perhaps I just missed Sulis; she was off with Myrddin supervising the stone haulers.

Uthne lay down on his fur-covered straw mattress, and I cleared some dirty clothing from a stool and sat down. He was in a good mood because he caught as many fish as I, and the mead spurred his enthusiasm.

"Oh, the times we used to have, Gwyr. Remember how we'd take those two sisters to the river and swim naked after we'd had our way with each of them? Of course, that was before you laid eyes on Sulis. I don't know how you can be satisfied with just one woman."

"It was you who encouraged me to pursue her," I reminded him.

"Yes, I wanted you to conquer the Monument Builder's daughter," he said. "But I didn't expect she would conquer you instead."

I didn't know what he was implying, so I kept silent.

"All this building at the Sacred Circle," he continued. "That's Sulis' ambition, not the Gwyr I know."

I was stunned to hear Uthne thought so little of me. Perhaps he still considered me a younger brother. "You're wrong," I said. "It was always my wish to carry on my father's work by continuing to build at the Sacred Circle. I'm lucky to have Sulis and Myrddin help me."

"That's one way to look at it," Uthne replied. I didn't like his mocking tone. "It seems to me, though, your father's work was completed before his death, when Myrddin raised the last of the doorways. Perhaps you want to keep building so you can continue to exact tribute from me and the other chiefs." He got up to pour himself another cup of mead, and then sat upright on his bed.

"You don't want for anything, despite the tribute you pay," I said, gesturing toward the wealth of goods filling his hut. "Building has brought prosperity to the Plain. Besides, the work unites the clans; that was my father's vision, too, and I honor it."

"What's the purpose in uniting the clans?" Uthne asked, in a louder voice than before. "My clan does well on its own as does Dur's and the others'. This talk of unity is all Sulis' idea." He was almost shouting now.

Hurt that Uthne did not credit me for my own beliefs, I rose from the stool and began pacing. Action always helped me think more clearly. "You're wrong again, Uthne," I said. "Uniting the clans is my idea. Sulis' circle design just makes my idea visible to the people."

Uthne sighed. "Oh, yes, the people," he said, no longer shouting. "The people don't control my clan, I do. My priest and I determine what ceremonies my clan needs. Chiefs Dur, Oben, and Ferg are getting older, so Sulis' new idea of rebirth of their spirits appeals to them. But I don't want Sulis and her albino priest interfering with my decisions. That Querke does not honor my clan's rituals; he will do or say whatever Sulis asks him, just so he can be close to your power, Gwyr."

I stopped pacing. I suspected Querke's motives as well, but I wasn't about to admit that to Uthne. Instead, I replied, "It's better for me to have the power than the priests."

Uthne rose and squinted at me. "You've changed, Gwyr," he said.

I wanted to tell him he hadn't, that he was still the same spoiled and selfish boy he'd always been. Instead, I replied, "Yes, I've changed. For the better, I think."

Uthne snorted. "Sulis has got you so wrapped up in her spell you've lost your senses," he said.

I walked toward him until I was less than an arm's length away. "Perhaps you are jealous of me, as you've always been. Perhaps you haven't changed at all."

"And I won't," Uthne stated. "Despite the foolish thoughts Sulis is filling you with while you are filling her up. Build what you wish at the Sacred Circle; my clan is separate and will stay separate."

I turned and left his hut without another word. Uthne called after me, "Sulis is leading you down the wrong path, my friend. You'll be sorry."

I strode on, not turning to answer him. Sulis had warned me Uthne feared the loss of power that would come when the people could see the completed stone circle, symbol of one united Clan. I understood now that she was right. Unlike the other chiefs, Uthne wouldn't give up power in exchange for wealth or the promise of rebirth. Uthne wanted power in this lifetime. As such, he was a worthy rival, as I now saw he had always been, despite our friendship. But there could be only one Chief of All the Clans, and it would not be Uthne.

Myrddin

I am happy to have lived to see this day, for today I watched the first lintel raised for Sulis' stone circle. She is just twenty-one sun cycles, as old as I was when I first came to this place. Little did I know then that I would never leave Yula's Plains, now Gwyr's, or that I would be a father, let alone a father to such a daughter. For Sulis has surpassed me in her skills. She has placed the uprights perfectly, so that the space between them is half the width of the uprights themselves, a beautiful proportion. She takes great care in determining where the uprights are placed, so that each reflects the size and shape of the one opposite. The effect is very pleasing to the eye, and something I myself would not have considered. Maybe it's the woman's touch.

Just as I adapted a carpenter's trick to attach the lintels to the uprights of Yula's doorways, she has borrowed another carpenter's method to attach the lintels to each other. Her stone shapers have curved the lintels, so that when joined, they will form a circle of continuous stone atop the uprights, a greater accomplishment than the doorways I built. I can see it now, even with just the first lintel raised, how men and women will regard this most magnificent monument the world has yet seen—even more magnificent than the Great Tomb on the Boinna River—with wonder and awe and respect.

The Sacred Circle has become a noisy place. Rocks scrape against stone, as the finishers form perfect shaping. Haulers sing their work songs to keep pulling in unison. Foremen bellow orders to their crews, who curse just as loudly as they raise the uprights. The male smell of sweat and dirt fouls the air, and cleansing rains are always welcome. At first, the work crews looked only to me for instructions, but Sulis soon won their confidence with her skill as a builder and her concern for their safety. Except for my reliance on Rudgawr, I always held myself apart from the clansmen, but Sulis acts differently toward them. She treats them with respect, perhaps because they are, after all, her mother's people. In return, even the youngest of the crews, the ones who have not yet learned to respect the power of women, defer to her authority.

It amazes me how she can set so many men to work at the same time and keep track of their progress. I admit I can't always follow her complicated plans. While the stone hauling was far from completed, she began to erect the uprights. After the first grouping of uprights had settled for one cycle, she immediately set yet another crew to work building the earthen ramps to raise this first lintel. I give her credit; she was right to get the uprights and lintel raised before the hauling was completed. It inspires the men to work harder when they can see the results of their work. When the stone hauling is almost finished, she plans to assign the haulers to crews raising the uprights.

When I was her age, I wasn't so knowing, but then I didn't have myself as a teacher. I must have been a good one. At her age, I was lying with Ine, the lustiest woman I have ever known, and unknown to me, making this child. It's time for Sulis to have a child, before she gets too old. It's one thing for a man to become a father for the first time later in life, as I did, but not a woman. I have overheard Uthne joking about Sulis' infertility and Gwyr's—and he claims to be Gwyr's best friend! Besides, I would like a grandson to keep me company in my old age, to teach as I taught his mother. Now I understand why Ogwyn kept Sulis so close to her, much to my regret. But what if I had a granddaughter? Could there ever be another girl child like Sulis?

I fear I will not live to see my grandchild. Already my eyes are failing. I can see at great distances as well as I ever could, maybe better. I can see the eyes of a rabbit on the other side of the river, or the feathers of a bird roosting high in a tree. But somehow I cannot see objects close at hand. Small items, especially, like berries or nuts, appear blurred. And I've lost my taste for women. There are few who have lived as long as me, and those closest to my age are worn out from childbearing and usually toothless! Only a young woman could stir my passions now, and it would be undignified to have a woman younger than my daughter. I still have my work as a Monument Builder, but Sulis is the true Monument Builder of the stone circle.

Just as my instruction prepared Sulis to design her grand monument, Ogwyn's instruction prepared her well for her new role as priestess. I have never paid much attention to religion. When I was a boy studying at the site of the Great Tomb, we learned the fickle ways of the priests who let the tombs fall to establish their power over the Monument Builders. Since those days, we builders tried to keep our distance from the interfering priests whenever possible. After all, how can you win an argument with religion, which cannot be measured and tested as monuments are? What's true for the priests is simply what they say is true.

I was fortunate to have Yula as my patron, because he envied the priests' power and so did little to support their demands on us Monument Builders. And Gwyr has turned out to be a better chief than I would have predicted; he knows his limitations and wisely married my capable daughter. But he is not content to merely withhold his support from the priests as his father did. Instead, he wants to usurp their power and influence, and he knows Sulis has the imagination and the toughness to do just that.

I never put much stock in Ogwyn's ranting about the moon and the dead, but I must say Sulis' new idea about a man's spirit surviving death, and being reborn, has great appeal. Maybe it's just my age. As I'm nearing the time of death myself, the idea of another Myrddin building more monuments on this Plain generations from now—well, I find that very comforting. So I am going to take part in her new ceremony at the Sacred Circle next spring and fill my beaker cup. It's the least I can do for my daughter and Gwyr. The local people on this Plain are a superstitious lot. I've overheard their stories that I made the stones fly in the air like birds. They admire me, and fear me, too. By participating in Sulis' ritual, I will be acknowledging the power of her magic over mine. If she is correct and my spirit is reborn, I will come back to make these locals admire and fear me even more. But what if her religion is just another lie, and I am dead forever? Well, I will have lost nothing by submitting to her ceremony.

But this other idea of hers and Gwyr's, doing away with the five clans and forming one group of people, causes me great concern. I sense danger in it, and I don't know why. Maybe it's too new a concept for an old man like me. For generations, each chief has seen to the needs of his own clan, settling disputes among his clansmen and women, making provisions for orphaned children, and hiring Monument Builders to build his tomb. Sometimes a clan raided another's cattle and fighting ensued, but usually they were at peace, each clan on its own lands. It has been ever thus on these Plains, on this island, and even on my home island, which I left so many years ago.

When the chiefs agreed to join forces to rebuild the Sacred Circle, they empowered Yula to settle disputes that sometimes arose as the men from different clans worked together for the first time; but each chief retained his traditional authority within his own clan. This arrangement does not satisfy Sulis. She wants Gwyr to be the true leader of all five clans, with the chiefs carrying out his orders rather than giving their own. I don't think a chief like Uthne will want to take orders from anyone, even his friend Gwyr. Sulis says if the people follow her religion and believe their spirits will live again, perhaps in another clan, there will be no need for separate clans, and the chiefs will be forced to follow Gwyr. In this way, she says she will be building one people from the five clans, a kind of human monument that will stand longer and appear more powerful than even the stone circle she and I are building.

"The spiritual idea behind the stone circle, Father," she told me as we walked the worksite, "is more important that the stones themselves. My monument and my rituals will unite the five clans into one people who share the same beliefs, who honor the ancestors with the moon and build their wealth with the sun. By joining their energies of body and mind, the united people will learn more, achieve more, and possess more than any one clan chief can imagine."

If power were her goal, as it is Gwyr's, I could better understand her actions. I am a man of the physical world. I understand earth and stone, the movements of the sun and moon, rich ornaments of gold and copper, things I can see and measure. I don't understand why she wants to give birth to this union of the clans.

Gwyr

Sulis is pregnant at last, and I am thankful she has finally consented to bear my child. She promised me that, before the ninth lintel of her circle was raised, I would see her belly bulge, and now it is so. I am hoping for a son, to guide and mold and instruct, as my father and Myrddin did me. Myrddin says there is nothing like a daughter to make a man's heart burst with pride. Sulis asks for neither, just offers her prayers to the moon goddess for a healthy baby who will survive the dangers of coming into the world. As medicine woman, she knows how to prepare for the birth. She takes a mixture of herbs at every meal and is training the serving girl Lena in midwifery.

Our crops and herds share in her fertility, fish crowd the River Av and game abounds in our forests. The people believe her pregnancy has brought new prosperity to all the chiefs, including Uthne. I once thought he would be the one I could count on the most. Instead, he became my rival. Perhaps I should have expected that, as we are close in age. I rarely see him anymore, but I've been told he envies the upcoming birth of my child. Chiefs Dur, Oben, and Ferg, although not quite as old as Myrddin, have lived long enough to find Sulis' new religious rituals of rebirth very appealing. Not Uthne. He wants his power in this lifetime; even his increasing wealth does not satisfy him.

Although the child growing inside has calmed and quieted Sulis, she does not ignore the progress of the building. Already, fifteen uprights and nine lintels of her stone circle have been raised to enclose the tallest doorway and the two moon doorways on either side of it, where she will hold her rebirthing ritual. Myrddin, giddy at the thought of being a grandfather, would much prefer to see his daughter lying in her bed for the next several months, instead of continuing with her work. But she is determined to conduct her first ceremony at the Sacred Circle on the first full moon following the Even Day when spring begins. By then, she says, she will be one full moon away from the birth of my child.

* * * *

On the evening of Sulis' rebirthing ceremony, she stood before the tallest of my father's doorways, her belly big and low. It was easy to imagine a spirit of the dead ancestors being born again through her body. At the edge of the incomplete circle of stones, our clansmen stood as witnesses. Querke, near the moonrise doorway, lit a pile of herbs; their sweet smell wafted in the air and made me lightheaded. Before the moonset doorway, Sulis' priests played drums and sang, while her priestesses fetched water from the ditch surrounding the circle and danced a story of death and rebirth.

As the light of the full moon filled the Sacred Circle, she slowly walked to the moonrise doorway. We initiates followed: myself; then chiefs Dur, Oben and Ferg with their lifemates; then Myrddin. Each man carried a decorated cup, symbolic of the womb in which his spirits would be reborn, filled with his own bodily fluids. My eyes searched for Uthne, but he had apparently chosen not to participate.

She poured life-giving water into my cup, lifted it up to the moon goddess and prayed, "Watch over and protect the future generations of the people of the Plain, that they may find strength in unity and know they are reborn as one people, in spirit and in body." Then she instructed me to spill the contents of my cup onto the earth. She repeated this rite with each initiate, ending with Myrddin.

Just as she was finishing her prayer, Uthne's voice rang out. He was standing on the causeway just outside the earthwork circle, where no stone uprights had yet been raised. Although he must have had a clear view of us, with the moonlight behind, he himself was partly hidden in the darkness.

"No," he roared. "We are five clans, not one people, and no child will be born from this false priestess so Gwyr can take my power as chief."

I didn't realize what was happening next, but Myrddin's senses were sharp and alert. Even in the dark and at a distance, he must have seen Uthne raise a bow and arrow and point them in Sulis' direction. As the last initiate, Myrddin had been left standing closest to her. In the moment between my breaths, time stopped. I heard the whoosh of an arrow flying past. I saw Myrddin hurl himself in front of his daughter, my priestess, and then fall, an arrow in his throat.

I called for my clansmen to bring me weapons, and was pleased to hear the chiefs call out for their hatchets, daggers, bows and arrows as well. Sulis was kneeling beside Myrddin with her ear to his chest, listening for a heartbeat, but I could see the arrow had stopped his breathing. She looked up at me, with an expression not of grief, but of revenge. I ran along the causeway and the chiefs followed, as did Sulis, moving faster than I would have thought possible with her big belly.

"Stop, I heard a sound behind us," said Dur, and as we turned, we saw Uthne fleeing to the west. We shot our arrows, and two landed, one in his side and one in his chest, but he remained standing and lunged sideways. Suddenly, he was hit from behind, an arrow straight through the back on his left side, landing directly into his heart. He fell on his face, and I turned to see which one of us had killed him. It was Sulis. Still holding her bow, she strode to Uthne's body and stomped her foot on his back, splitting the arrow that protruded.

"Leave him where he fell," she commanded. "Leave him for the wolves and the birds. He will not be buried like a clansman. His spirit is not worthy to be reborn."

Sulis

After I killed Uthne, the birthing water poured from my body. Too early, I thought, my time was one full moon away, but the shock to my body of Myrddin's death precipitated the flow. Just as my mother entered the world of the dead on the day I was born, so my father entered the world of the dead on the day I gave birth.

Gwyr, always at his best at times requiring fast action, sensed what was happening without my saying a word and acted without any apparent thought. My lifemate, about to become a father, lifted me up and carried me back to our compound. He called for Lena, the midwife I had trained myself, and then left us to the work that only women do. I was prepared for the pain I had seen other women experience. I knew how to take my mind away from it, as Ogwyn taught me so long ago.

Lena placed a stick in my mouth and I bit it hard as I pushed down into my womb, over and over until I felt a strong life force expel itself from my body.

"Gwyr has his son," said Lena, and I heard his cry, loud and demanding. But the pain had not left yet. "It's just the blood after birthing that's coming," Lena said, but at that moment I realized she was wrong.

All through my pregnancy, I had dreams of two—two flowers in the field, two birds flying into the sun, two fish in the river—but, preoccupied with my rituals, I had not paid attention to them. Another series of tightening pains began, and this time, I felt a feminine energy emerge. I knew my second child was a girl even before Lena announced it to me.

A boy for the sun and a girl for the moon, living omens to dispel any doubts—if there were more doubters like Uthne—that the gods favored my new religion and my stone circle monument. I examined each of my babies as I washed them in turn. Although perfect, beautiful, no birthmarks, with all their fingers and toes, neither had the red hair of the Monument Builders. The boy, the bigger of the two, looked like Gwyr, only bald. The girl, wiry, with a shock of dark hair, brought to life my mind picture of the mother I had never seen. I wondered whose spirits had been reborn in them, and hoped Myrddin lived on in one of my babies, but it was too soon to tell.

Lena called for Gwyr to enter the hut. When he saw me lying in bed with a naked baby in each arm, the astonished look on his face made me laugh despite the pain I was feeling from the birthing and from my father's death.

"Sulis, you've surprised me again. A son and a daughter, all at once. You must be all right, if you can laugh. It's a good thing I thought of a girl's name, just in case," he said, for it is the father's right to name the children. "The girl will be called Evie and the boy, Myrddin."

At the sound of my father's name, I started to cry, tears of grief but also of joy, because of Gwyr's kindness in naming his son after my father. Gwyr held all three of us in his arms, and then asked Lena to take the babies to their own bed. "Sulis needs to rest. It's been a terrible and wonderful night."

"I must make plans for Myrddin's burial," I said, as I drank the seeds to start my milk flowing.

"Tomorrow," Gwyr answered. "And tomorrow I will tell the chiefs and the people of my power to father two children at once." He talked as if he did all the work, not me!

My last thought before sleep overcame me was that my babies were fortunate to have each other. As a child I had no siblings, no mother and a father who was often absent.

The next morning, Gwyr sent messengers to all the villages, to tell the people of Uthne's treachery, Myrddin's heroic death, and the birth of our sun-and-moon twins. Gwyr moved quickly to secure his power by making Dur's son Enda chief of Uthne's clan. None of the other chiefs objected, nor did

Uthne's people, who realized his sacrilege at the Sacred Circle brought shame on their families.

By afternoon, I was back on my feet, seeing to Myrddin's funeral. I myself anointed his body—thankfully someone had removed the arrow from his throat and dressed him in the fine woolen tunic and cloak the brotherhood of Monument Builders wore. In the stiffening fingers of his right hand, I placed his prized possession, his bronze measuring rod.

Just before sunset, the funeral procession, led by Gwyr and me, made its way to the burial site, a hill overlooking the Sacred Circle. I held the beaker I had given my father at the rebirthing ceremony just the evening before. Foremen from the work crews carried Myrddin's body on a wooden pallet, followed by Rudgawr, Querke, and his guide. Rudgawr walked with great difficulty, and I marveled my father, so much stronger, had been taken by death before his sickly friend. Querke carried a heavy axe, the only task I had assigned him. I intended to conduct this burial ritual entirely on my own and use the axe in the ceremony.

Our clansmen stayed in the village. Although the rebirthing rituals were public events, only the closest family and friends attended a burial. So when we got to the top of the hill, I was surprised to see the four chiefs standing to one side of the awaiting gravediggers.

"It is right that you are here with us," Gwyr told them. "Because our clans are now as one."

I directed the foremen to lay Myrddin's body flat on its back, with his feet pointing to the circle, as if at any time he would sit up and see before him the magnificent doorways he had built. Overcome with emotion, both from seeing my father's lifeless form and from the waves of feeling that childbirth brings, I nevertheless knew that, as Gwyr's priestess, I must complete the ritual. Placing the beaker alongside the body, I murmured the same prayer as the night before, but this time directed to the spirit of my father, as well as to the moon goddess: "Watch over and protect the future generations of the people of the Plain, that they may find strength in unity and know they are reborn as one people, in spirit and in body."

I added, "May the spirit of Myrddin, the great Monument Builder of the Sacred Circle, live again through the newborn body of a clan baby." Then I took the axe and placed it near his right shoulder. "In the spirit of Myrddin, I bury this axe, to symbolize that all feelings of hatred his murder has aroused are now being buried with him." The chiefs gasped at my prayers, and Dur held back tears, but I said no more. I had come to the end of my strength.

Moved himself, Gwyr stepped forward and tore off his new gold plate, with its hook to hold his dagger, and placed it on Myrddin's body, as a sign of respect. Then Dur laid his prized copper dagger, its wooden handle decorated with tiny gold pins, by my father's side. Oben, Ferg, and Enda followed, each taking a valued object from his own person and leaving it near the body—a jadeite axe, flint arrowheads, a fine leather wristguard. My father had more precious wealth in death than he ever knew in life.

Then the diggers covered the body with earth, to protect it from the birds and the animals. By the next full moon, a huge mound would be built over my father's body, as a further sign of respect. Only then did the building of the stone circle continue.

The story does not end with the birth of Sulis' twins and Myrddin's burial, dear reader. There is more to tell. I must hurry now. I hear the rumble of the approaching Roman troops.

Maeve Haley's Blog

What the Archaeological Evidence Tells Us
Posted August 25

Is the Helen of Troy story true? Although archaeologists have discovered the ruins of ancient Troy, no one can say with certainty that the events described in the romantic legend actually occurred. Similarly, who can vouch for the accuracy of Oisin's story, passed down through generations and only recently revealed? Still, the known archaeological evidence does, indeed, confirm several parts of the story told in these scrolls.

For example, the Salisbury Museum, south of Stonehenge, exhibits an ancient skeleton found in the ditch there and shot with arrows, just as the scrolls describe Uthne's death. Another skeleton of a tall man buried with magnificent burial goods was found when one of the mounds near Stonehenge was excavated. Archaeologists have always assumed it was the local chieftain because of the extravagance of the gold, copper, and bronze objects buried with him. But their description is virtually identical to the scroll's account of Myrddin's burial.

Twins
Posted August 27

If the birth of Sulis' twins sounds familiar, it may be because another great female ruler of the ancient world also bore twins, a boy and a girl, whom she named after the sun and the moon: Cleopatra. Perhaps Cleopatra simply plagiarized Sulis' history. More likely, the Druids knew about Cleopatra's twins and appropriated that detail to embroider Sulis' story. Or perhaps the story is true for both women. After all, it's still fashionable among Hollywood stars today to give birth to twins, sometimes with the help of modern medical technology.

Scroll XI

Sulis

Querke came to see me a few days after Myrddin's death. I was resting in bed with my twins by my side, my energy drained by birth and death.

"The clansmen and women can't stop talking about what happened," Querke said, as his weak eyes peered into the faces of my children. Satisfied the babies were well, he continued, "But even after Uthne's treachery, your father's death and the birth of these beautiful twins, they speak most about the axe you buried with your father. They say any jealousies that existed among the clans were buried with that axe."

"I hope that differences have been buried as well, so we can unite as one Clan," I said without moving from my bed. "And I'm pleased the people approve."

"More than approve," Querke replied. "Uthne's clansmen want to carve axe-heads on one of the doorway stones, to commemorate your forgiveness. They asked me to speak to you about it."

Immediately I felt some of my strength returning and sat up to consider this request. What would Myrddin have answered? I missed my father. I knew having this symbol of unity carved in stone would justify Gwyr's bid for power, but did not want to admit this to Querke.

"Yes," I told Querke, "I would like to see that, but not for my own sake. Myrddin battled the great-stones to build those doorways, so it is fitting he be remembered there."

And so, even as the mound of dirt and rocks was still being heaped over my father's body, Gwyr and I stood inside the Sacred Circle and watched as Uthne's clansmen pounded and chipped their carvings into a doorway stone, their hard work reparation for Uthne's crime.

When I finally resumed building my monument, I felt Myrddin's spirit guide me. Not only was I working to honor both the old ways and my new religion, to unite the clans and consolidate Gwyr's power, but also to honor my father, who was often in my thoughts. Now I would need all the skills he taught me to execute my complex design, one that had never been tried before. Although I was confident of my ability, I missed being able to seek out Myrddin's advice. There were no other Monument Builders on the Plain to consult, as my father had had with Corna. Success depended entirely on my knowledge and intuition. I came to realize that, just as my new religion also preserved Ogwyn's old ways, I would have to develop new techniques to improve on the Monument Builders' methods.

As the work continued, my twins grew, and I vowed to celebrate their birth-days as my father had celebrated mine. By their first birth-day, the stone hauling was finished; all the stones I would need for the uprights and lintels were now on the Plain near the Sacred Circle. I took careful measurements of the great-stones and had the stone finishers mark each with a special sign to indicate where it would be used. For the ritual I had in mind, I needed to ensure the ring of lintels, once raised, would be level. This would be difficult to achieve, for Myrddin had told me Yula's priests forbade Fluj from completely leveling the ground of the Sacred Circle. So for the uprights that would be placed where the ground sloped slightly downward I selected the tallest stones. To be level, the lintels had to be close to the same thickness, too, so I chose stones of a similar size and sent these off to the stone shapers and finishers to round into curves.

Gwyr, who had since boyhood sought out Myrddin's counsel, now turned to Chief Dur, who became a trusted ally. With Dur's support, Gwyr convinced the other chiefs to supply more men and boys for the work crews. Dur's son Enda, now chief of Uthne's clan, was the first to agree. Chief Ferg and Chief Oben seemed content to accede to Gwyr's leadership; neither displayed Uthne's desire for power. Oben was too busy with his many women and Ferg, too fond of his mead.

With bigger crews, we made visible progress, and as a result, I sensed enthusiastic support from the foremen, although, being a woman, I never became as friendly with them as Myrddin had with Rudgawr. Perhaps they also feared me a little and respected me more after I executed Uthne. At least that was Lena's assessment. Her duties as a midwife finished, at least for the time being, with the birth of my twins, Lena stayed on as their nursemaid, tending to the babies while I directed the building at the Sacred Circle.

At times the problems and challenges that arose made me wish I could trade places with Lena. Since the uprights were of different heights, their foundation holes had to be of different depths in order to achieve a level surface for the lintels. It took a lot of measuring before and after the holes were dug. Once an upright cracked after it was struck by lightning. The same thing happened when my father was building Yula's doorways. He told me about it many times.

"Gwyr insisted I use that stone, and so far it has held. It may hold for generations yet to come, but, Sulis, we Monument Builders should have higher standards," Myrddin had warned. I decided to follow my father's example rather than his words, and instructed the foreman to pack the hole with flint and chalk to support the damaged stone.

I often took my wooden model to the Sacred Circle with me, along with pieces of slate and chalk. Although the model showed uprights of equal width, in truth the great-stones were irregular, despite the abilities of the stone shapers. To keep my design pleasing to the eye, I decided to space the uprights the same distance apart from center to center. These adjustments to the design required me to calculate and recalculate on my chalkboard before the crews could raise the uprights in the exact positions I determined. Each upright had to settle for at least one sun cycle before receiving its lintels, so I also had to remember the season when each had been raised. Shortly after my twins' third birth-day, all the uprights in my circle—and some of the lintels—were standing.

To make sure the lintels were level around the circle, I used the Monument Builder's tool my father had given me and that he called a square. Made of wood, it resembled a doorway with one upright missing. Attached to it was a thin rope from which hung a small rock, no bigger than my fist. Standing on a ramp, I held the square by its upright and when the rope hung straight down, I could look over the top of the tool and sight the correct height of the lintels.

I also devised a long pottery basin with wooden handles on each end and a straight line incised around its interior. The workmen filled this basin with water and placed it on the top of the lintel as they maneuvered it into place. If the water stayed level with the line, they knew the lintel was level; if the water in the basin was uneven, they knew they had to raise the lintel even higher—a difficult but not impossible job of levering the great-stone and adding flint and chippings under it—or call in the stone finishers to lower the height by pounding the top of the uprights.

Construction continued from the Even Day in the spring until the second full moon after the Even Day in the fall. I released the work crews in the winters. Not only was the earth too frozen to dig, but as medicine woman, I feared for the workers' safety on the slick ground. Besides, Gwyr wanted to encourage the clansmen to celebrate the winter sunset, in Yula's honor, with five days of rest and feasting. And I wanted to spend time with my children, away from the work sites.

As the fifth birth-day of my children approaches, my son Myrddin, tall and strong, wins races and excels at all games, so like his father in every way. Gwyr beams with pride at his athletic son, but little Evie, eager to please, brings joy to his life. She is already learning my plants, as I did with Ogwyn, and tells me she wants to be a medicine woman like me and the great-grandmother she never knew. Neither of my twins shows the signs of a Monument Builder, nor do I see my father's spirit in them. They were born too near his death, his spirit not yet free to be reborn. And so I must have another child. Soon, at the festival Gwyr and I will hold once the Stone Circle is completed, I will conceive again.

* * * *

"There must be fertility rites, music, dancing, and feasting," Querke said, as together we devised ceremonies to dedicate the monument. We met in my planting hut, during the winter before the last of the lintels would be raised. "And to please Gwyr, we must honor the sun, but we cannot forget the moon," Querke reminded me. I knew he was right, but I also knew the rites he wanted would not be enough. The dedication had to be more than a religious ritual; it had to prove to the people that Gwyr was Chief of All the Clans of the Plain.

As if hearing my thoughts, Querke said, "Look to the moon for guidance, Sulis."

The next day, I went to the Sacred Circle, deserted in the cold air, and walked the rectangle formed by the four stones laid by the Master Builder, my father's teacher. As I followed this path of moonrises and moonsets, sunrises and sunsets, I remembered what my father taught me about their cycles. I lay down within the womb formed by my father's five doorways and let the earth energies enter my body. After the sun set, I rose and walked to one of the middle height doorways and peered through it to follow the rising of the moon. I remembered my father sharing with me the most secret of the Monument Builders' teachings: how to know when the moon was going to disappear from the sky, not merely hide behind a cloud, but vanish completely. And then the direct knowing came to me. I raced back to my hut and grabbed a slate and chalk and made some quick calculations that confirmed my conclusion. Could it be? I erased the chalk and began my sums again, more carefully now, plotting the numbers as Myrddin had taught me. Yes, it was so.

What a glorious ceremony it was going to be! I long ago planned that Gwyr and I would walk atop the ring of lintels, a stunning display of our power, but now I had another even more compelling sight to show the people. The moon was my ally. I told no one except Gwyr what I had foreseen. He did not doubt my prediction.

"Sulis," he said, "you are truly my priestess."

Not even Querke knew what I had in mind; I told him only of our plan to walk the lintels and asked him to prepare some soothing chants to accompany us.

But for my plan to work, the construction had to be done before my birthday. I would have to bring the crews back before the Even Day and drive them to work more quickly than they had since my father raised the last of Yula's doorways.

* * * *

The day I had been awaiting for eleven sun cycles finally arrived. My entire life has been devoted to this monument, and my children daily prove, if I needed convincing, that my life is passing too quickly. The monument I envisioned as a girl, and built as a woman with the power of my children's father, is finished. The dirt ramp built to raise the last lintel has been cleared away, and the worksite at the Sacred Circle tidied up. I sent the crews home, so I could be alone with the circle of stones I created.

Looking at it for the first time—without workers and wooden poles and stone tools scattered around the site—satisfied me. My stone circle dominated the Plain, as I intended. My father told me of tombs and monuments built overlooking the sea or near beautiful lakes, but here nothing detracted from my creation. Although many stone circles have been built before, none have my lintels to connect the stones and reflect the perfect shapes of the sun and the moon. Over the years as the monument was being built, I had seen it glow in the moonlight and shine in the sunlight, but I liked it best on cloudy days like this one, when even the gray skies did not overpower my enormous stones.

I entered the circle between the two uprights with the widest space separating them, passing under their connecting lintel. The energy concentrated inside the circle flowed into me. I felt the pride of giving birth. Standing in the center, with the five doorways now surrounding me as well, my eyes were drawn to the heavens through the tallest of Yula's and my father's doorways. I turned to look all around my circle. Power and awe radiated from the stones themselves. Generations from now, women and men will come to this place and see, set in stone, our knowledge of the sun and moon, our belief in life and rebirth, and our unity as a people.

* * * *

People from all the clans, Monument Builders from my father's home island, and even traders from far lands came to the festival to dedicate my circle capped by a ring of stones. All who saw it knew it marked the holy site of a great people. There is no other like it, and even the Monument Builders who attended admitted that none have the skills to build another. To honor the sun that gives life to our crops, the festival began at sunrise on the longest day of the year, my birth-day. As the sun rose between the two uprights that formed the entrance to the circle, priestesses entered the ancient site, took off their robes, and danced naked around the stones. Faster and faster they danced, to capture the energy flowing from the sun, while the priests chanted and played their drums and pipes.

To bless the sacred ground anew, after sunset that day, Gwyr and I lay on the ground at the center of the Sacred Circle and joined our bodies. We were hidden by the darkness, the doorways, and the circle of stones, while the people stood outside the earthworks and clapped and whistled their approval. When we finished, I felt the hot union of our lovemaking take hold inside me and knew at once life bloomed within me again.

The festival lasted five days and nights, with feasting, of course, and mead mixed with cooked hemp. I brewed special liquids that improved virility when drunk by a man and stirred a woman's passions when rubbed into her skin. At sunset on the third day, the circle was open for all clansmen and women to enjoy in the same way Gwyr and I had, and many did, thus assuring the fertility of our lands for generations to come.

On the last day of the festival, Gwyr ordered fires to be lit and mead to be poured, and we heard the shouts of happy revelers continuing as darkness fell. Shortly before sunset, as the full moon rose in the sky, Gwyr and I climbed on ladders and platforms until we reached the top of the ring of lintels. The crowd hushed and I could feel their eyes upon us. Then Gwyr and I walked completely around the circle, as the clans cheered and whistled below. We stopped, and I prayed loudly from atop the lintels with Gwyr beside me.

"By the power of this stone circle, which honors both the sun and the moon, your spirits will be reborn. Future generations of the clans of the Plain will carry your spirit," I proclaimed.

And Gwyr added, "You will be reborn because we are one people now. And one people need one Chief."

Then, according to the secret cycles known only to Monument Builders, the moon began to hide herself in the sky, as I predicted she would, as I had told Gwyr she would. By the light of the bonfires, I saw the people huddled in the darkness below us. When the moon had completely vanished, some women screamed and some men began to run away, but Querke and his priests stopped them with sacred chants that soothed the panic.

I cried out to the darkness, "This great stone circle honors the sun, but also remembers the moon, lest she desert us. For it is through the moon the spirits of the dead are born again into the one united people of the Plain."

Gradually the moon began to reveal herself again in the sky, as I knew she must. Then, just as we had rehearsed, Gwyr declared, "By coming back to us, the moon gives her blessing to the united clans."

From below arose a voice I did not expect, that was not part of my plan. It was Querke's.

"The moon shines on Gwyr now as the one Chief of All the Clans of the Plain," he said. "One chief for one people." Querke's priests began to chant with him, "One chief for one people," and the clansmen joined in the refrain.

And so the dedication of the monument came to a close, and all recognized Gwyr as their leader.

Gwyr was pleased with the festival, for my new religion justified his power. And I was pleased as well, for I have preserved the old ways of the moon, as Ogwyn would have wanted, and added them to the new ways of the sun, for which my father built the five doorways. I have created one belief, one clan to whom the dead are reborn, and one Chief to rule over them, all represented in the one and only ringed circle of stones. It is not just what can be seen or touched that makes a people great. The things that are unseen—our beliefs about what is important or right or necessary—will unite our people into the future, an even greater monument, I think, than the stone circle itself.

Gwyr

Yesterday she called for Querke and told him how the burial rites were to be conducted. Then she slept a while. When she awoke again, wet from the fever, she spoke to me.

"Do not bury me with my amber pendant; dress me in the glass beads instead. Leave the amber to Evie, so that she will think of me always, as I thought of Ine."

Despite her weak body, her will was still strong, but mine was not. For the first time since Yula died, I wept. How my life had changed in just a few short days. Then I was a powerful chief, awaiting the birth of my third child. Now I have another son, and I pray to the sun god he will live and be strong. But Sulis will not survive his birth. Neither her medicines nor her priests can help her now. Nor can I. Our power is meaningless.

Sulis is pleased with the child. He was born with the thin skin of the womb covering his head. She carefully removed it.

"He must carry this womb-skin always, for it gives him power," she said. "Look, Gwyr, he has the look of Myrddin in his eyes. Myrddin never blamed me for the death of my mother. Do not blame this boy. Remember, he is part of me. Give him his name."

"I name him Canu. Our love lives in him, and in Myrddin and Evie."

She smiled and seemed content, but said no more. Before sunset, her spirit left her body.

I had known her for seventeen sun cycles. What would I have been without her? Her medicines saved my life and kept me strong. The stone circle was her idea, not mine, and it was she who built it. I never cared for religion, but by honoring the moon as well as the sun, she inspired the people. Her rituals and her monument united the clans, in a way I could not have with my cattle, and lands, and gold. Like a fool, I never once imagined I would ever be without her.

Already, the people are calling her a goddess. Some say a mother goddess, because she gave birth to our united clans with her rituals. Some say an earth goddess, because she cured with the plants of the earth. Or a moon goddess, because she made the moon vanish and appear again the night we dedicated the stone circle.

I will bury her near her monument with its thirty columns. Now they count not only the nights of the moon cycle, but also the thirty winters of her life.

And so Gwyr buried the Great Sulis just outside the Sacred Circle, where she could see her perfect Circle of Stones forever. No one since can be buried closer to her monument. Gwyr never took another lifemate or fathered more children. He was a good Chief, even kinder than before. Canu wore his womb-skin in a gold ball tied around his neck with a leather cord and grew in wisdom. All could see that the spirit of Myrddin lived on in him.

My story is done. I shall seal these scrolls in a bronze chest and take them with me on a boat to Myrddin's island, where even the Romans dare not venture.

Maeve Haley's Blog

Sulis' Grave?
Posted August 28

A small burial mound very close to the Stonehenge circle could very well be Sulis' gravesite.

Sex Inside the Stones
Posted August 29

Chad from New Orleans posts: "My favorite part of the story was when Gwyr and Sulis had sex to dedicate the monument. And the nude dancing."

Vases from 500 BC show ring dances of naked women, so it's not implausible that similar ceremonies were held at Stonehenge.

Magical rites involving sexual intercourse go back to the prehistoric era. Such practices have been linked to worshippers of Isis, Egyptian goddess of fertility and motherhood, and to the Eleusinian Mysteries of the ancient Greeks. Before the Christian era, kings often had to mate with a priestess before claiming the right to rule. Modern day followers of Wicca still practice what they call the Great Rite, often performed within a magic circle at seasonal festivals.

While many in the twenty-first century might consider such practices pornographic, the pre-Christian religions accepted them as powerful rituals.

So What Does Stonehenge Really Mean?
Posted August 30

Dan from Washington, D.C. posts: "So what does Stonehenge really mean? Is it a calendar or a temple? Or something else?"

You've asked the million dollar question, Dan. What's it all about?

Stonehenge was most likely the central gathering place that marked a clan's territory, and a reminder of the ongoing influence of their ancestors and of the importance of community, given the number of people it took to build it. A monument like Stonehenge may signify mankind's domination over nature, because it's an impressive structure made by men, not gods. Some scholars postulate it may also indicate a new perception of time, since it was meant to last forever.

Just think what that giant circle of ringed stone communicated to a pre-literate society. It symbolized power and unity, past beliefs and future aspirations. So in answer to your question, yes, it was both a temple and an astronomical observatory, and it was also something else, a courthouse, a meeting place, and a repository of all their collective knowledge. In our modern times, we expect categories and specialization, but Neolithic purposes were truly seamless. It was all one to them.

My personal opinion is that Stonehenge marked the beginnings of English civilization. That's why millions of visitors each year continue to be drawn to this ruined circle of ancient stones in the English countryside.

How Civilization Begins
Posted August 31

Several comments were posted yesterday after I wrote that Stonehenge marked the beginning of English civilization. Some questioned my opinion; others wanted to know more about why I feel this way. So here goes.

Why were families, tribes, and clans in some parts of the world able to put aside their individual interests and form states and countries, while in other parts of the world, even today, places like Iraq, or Bosnia, or even Northern Ireland, people still have difficulty progressing beyond tribal and ethnic loyalties for the greater good? When I was in graduate school, I read a study about a village that just couldn't seem to make any progress. The authors said that we incorrectly assume that if people have enough resources and knowledge, they will somehow just automatically advance and form a society, an organized effort to work for the common good, for any goal beyond the needs of the immediate family. But it *doesn't* automatically happen. First you need a common culture that defines the values, ethics and standards of a society; without common culture, there's no impetus to create or maintain any kind of organization.

Sulis created the culture, symbolized by Stonehenge. Of course priests and monuments existed way before her time, but she took it to the next level by combining the old ways with the new in her unique design and more powerful religious beliefs. She used religion to secure Gwyr's political power. In America, you hold to the separation of church and state, an ideal that

~ 129 ~

doesn't play in much of the rest of the world. The Queen of England is still head of the Church of England, in Ireland the so-called national schools are Catholic schools, and the ayatollahs wield power over Muslim governments.

So in a way, Sulis did start civilization in England by building not only a stone circle but also a common culture. I think civilization has more to do with the power of our intangible beliefs than with the tangible evidence—arrowheads, pottery shards, and the like—that fascinate so many of my fellow archaeologists.

Besides, remember that drink that accounted for Ogwyn's long life, the one Sulis made for Gwyr, Myrddin, and Querke from some kind of evergreen berries? I think they're juniper berries, and she was making gin, *the* major component of English civilization!

About the Author

In 2001, K.P. Robbins closed the Washington, DC, ad agency she founded, moved to Ireland, and began to write *The Stonehenge Scrolls.*

The idea for the novel had been brewing since her first visit to Stonehenge and Newgrange a dozen years earlier. "The first time I saw Stonehenge, I was hooked," she says.

Since then, she has "chased the stones," visiting and studying stone circles, dolmens, and cairns in England, Scotland, Wales, Brittany, and Ireland.

Her short stories have been published on *WashingtonPost.com* and in the *Anthology of Appalachian Writers, Appalachian Writers Guild Anthology,* and *Seven Hills Review.*

A graduate of the West Virginia University School of Journalism, she lives with her husband in West Virginia and is writing a memoir about the year they lived in Ireland.

* * * *

Did you enjoy The Stonehenge Scrolls? If so, please help us spread the word about K.P. Robbins and MuseItUp Publishing. It's as easy as:

•Recommend the book to your family and friends
•Post a review
•Tweet and Facebook about it

Thank you
MuseItUp Publishing

Acknowledgements

Writing is a solitary occupation, but the support of family, friends, and fellow writers makes completing a novel a less daunting task. Thanks, first of all, to my husband Bill, who has steadfastly inspired and encouraged me. My friends Pat, Marlene, Barbara, and June took the time to read and react to drafts. My writing group buddies Jim, Eric, Ken, George, B.J., Millie, Pam and Tara provided excellent feedback. Two novelists/writing teachers gently critiqued the manuscript; Leslie Pietrzyk reviewed an early draft and Priscilla Rodd, a close-to-final version. Without agent Jeanie Loiacono, publisher Lea Schizas and editors Nancy Bell and Judy Roth, the manuscript wouldn't have become a published novel. My deepest gratitude to you all.

MuseItUp Publishing
Where Muse authors entertain readers!
https://museituppublishing.com
Visit our website for more books for your reading pleasure.

You can also find us on Facebook:
http://www.facebook.com/MuseItUp
and on Twitter:
http://twitter.com/MusePublishing

CPSIA information can be obtained at www.ICGtesting.com
Printed in the USA
BVOW05s2140210115

384272BV00003B/494/P